Jake's Dragon

For,
Sue Bradshaw
James D. McFarland
5/3/2020

Jake's Dragon

Riano D. McFarland

Copyright © 2019 by Riano D. McFarland.

Library of Congress Control Number:	2019912419
ISBN: Hardcover	978-1-7960-5440-8
Softcover	978-1-7960-5439-2
eBook	978-1-7960-5438-5

All rights reserved. No part of this book may be reproduced or transmitted in any form or by any means, electronic or mechanical, including photocopying, recording, or by any information storage and retrieval system, without permission in writing from the copyright owner.

This is a work of fiction. Names, characters, places and incidents either are the product of the author's imagination or are used fictitiously, and any resemblance to any actual persons, living or dead, events, or locales is entirely coincidental.

Any people depicted in stock imagery provided by Getty Images are models, and such images are being used for illustrative purposes only.
Certain stock imagery © Getty Images.

Print information available on the last page.

Rev. date: 08/22/2019

To order additional copies of this book, contact:
Xlibris
1-888-795-4274
www.Xlibris.com
Orders@Xlibris.com
799903

CHAPTER 1

JAKE WAS EXCITED about the first day of summer break from school. What healthy eleven-year-old boy wouldn't be? Having packed all his fishing gear onto his bicycle the night before, he awoke and dressed at the crack of dawn, wrapped some leftover chicken and biscuits in a paper towel, and stuffed them into his backpack before darting out the back door and down the lane on his bike.

The lake was only about two miles behind his house, but the thick summertime foliage of the cedar, oak, and maple trees populating the forest separating them made Jake's preferred fishing cove nearly invisible until you were right on top of it.

That being said, the cove itself was a breathtaking sight to behold. The mist hovering above the surface of the lake would burn off instantly once the sun cleared the treetops, revealing a mirrorlike surface virtually free of waves and ripples.

Along the shores, the diversity of the surrounding forest gave way to a thick concentration of cedars, which, because of their density, had choked out most other species of trees and vegetation along the water's edge. As a result, the ground beneath the cedar canopy was rocky and often precarious to navigate.

Parking his bike in a small grassy area alongside a stream that flowed into the lake, Jake grabbed his fishing gear and made his way across the rocky terrain to his favorite fishing spot: an old rock wall that extended out into the lake about thirty feet from the shore.

For Jake, the first cast of the day was always the most exciting. His favorite lure, a black-and-white speckled rooster tail, was permanently attached to the line, so his fishing rod was always ready for action.

The first cast was a long one as the line spun off the spool with a familiar whirring sound, breaking the silence that preceded the quiet splash of the lure into the placid water. As he reeled in, water droplets adorning the fishing line glistened in the morning sun appearing above the tree line surrounding the peaceful cove. Jake repeated this process on autopilot over and over without any serious mental participation while taking in the tranquil beauty of this idyllic little cove.

Suddenly, he felt that familiar double tap on the rooster tail and reflexively raised his rod tip to set the hook. The immediate tensioning of the line vaporized the dangling water droplets as a largemouth bass broke the water thirty yards from him. The fight was on.

Keeping the rod tip high, as his father had taught him, he adjusted the drag wheel to keep the line tight while preventing the fish from snapping it. After several minutes of following the bass up and down the rocky shore, he was finally close enough to net the fish and carry it out of and away from the water.

Holding the slippery fish down atop one of the large stones scattered across the ground, Jake used a pair of needle-nose pliers to carefully remove the treble hook from its mouth. Picking it up with both hands, he lifted the exhausted largemouth bass up into the air, admiring the intricate details and unique patterns of the scales along its back and sides.

After scrutinizing the fish for several minutes and from several different angles in the light of the morning sun, Jake walked back down to the water, releasing it into the lake at the exact spot where he'd landed it. It took a moment for the fish to realize it'd been freed, and upon that realization, it jetted back out into the cool deep waters of Old Hickory Lake.

Jake gathered his fishing gear and backpack and then returned to the grassy area beside the stream where he'd parked his bicycle. The remainder of his morning, he spent with his sketchbook and colored art pencils in hand, recreating in painstaking detail the image of the fish he'd caught and released earlier.

His tendency to block out every distraction and single-mindedly concentrate on a specific task at hand was something that made other children of his age very uncomfortable around him. The fact that he had never shared the products of these trancelike detours from society left them clueless as to the depth of his cognitive and artistic abilities.

Jake sketched astoundingly accurate, lifelike images of every fish he had ever caught. Within mere minutes, he could visually analyze any object, person, or animal and then produce artistic renderings of them that were so clear, they could easily be mistaken for photographs.

His "fishing" sketchbook was filled with remarkably vivid drawings of bass, bluegill, crappie, catfish, carp, stripers, and even a turtle he'd once snagged by mistake. His ever-present backpack was stuffed tightly with art supplies and other sketchbooks designated for various subjects such as clouds, birds, landscapes, wild animals, trees, flowers, cars, people, buildings, insects and arachnids, and even ghosts.

After finishing the drawing of the day's catch, he put away his sketchbook and pencils and then pulled out the chicken and biscuits he'd grabbed for lunch on his way out the door.

Gazing out across the lake, Jake watched the sunlight reflecting from the ripples in the water, whipped up by a light summer breeze. He smiled at the sight as the caps of each little wave glistened like diamonds.

Beyond the water, on the opposite side of the cove, he saw it, sprawled out along the rocky floor of the forest a few yards back from the shore. It was well camouflaged and nearly invisible as it blended in with the large black and gray stones surrounding it. The blotches of shade created by the canopy of cedar trees added the crowning touch, creating a near-perfect disguise for what appeared to be a truly massive creature.

Near perfect . . .

Jake leaned back on his elbows with his legs crossed at the ankles, watching the creature for several minutes while eating the lunch he'd brought with him, his eyes mostly hidden behind his baseball cap.

Mostly hidden . . .

The creature, with its fiery eyes barely even open, seemed to be assessing whether or not the young boy across the cove had actually noticed him. Like a chameleon, it could easily blend in with any natural surface. The only part of its body it couldn't change were the golden eyes it attempted to minimize by keeping them nearly shut.

Jake wasn't fooled. He knew exactly what he was looking at, but nothing in his demeanor betrayed that knowledge to the creature watching him from across the cove.

Jake finished his lunch and collected the paper towels, water bottle, and chicken bones he'd brought with him, leaving nothing behind, as his father had emphasized to him on many occasions. Mounting his bike and slinging his backpack onto his shoulders, Jake nonchalantly peddled his bike back up the road to his house as if nothing out of the ordinary had even happened.

Silently greeting his mom and dad as he came in through the back screen door, Jake rushed up the stairs to his bedroom, smiling. Today he'd start his new sketchbook: "Dragons."

CHAPTER 2

FOR MOST PEOPLE, such a close encounter with a dragon would have been terrifying, but for Jake, it was just another natural wonder hiding in plain sight. He'd seen many things in his rather brief lifetime that others had simply overlooked or downright failed to recognize. When trying to point them out, he'd either been laughed at and ridiculed or, even worse, ignored completely.

For Jake, explaining these things to others was like trying to describe the color purple to someone who'd been color-blind since birth. After a while, he'd learned to keep quiet about his more extraordinary encounters, and with no one to talk to about them, he grew more and more silent; sometimes he didn't speak at all.

Of all the things Jake had encountered, this was the most amazing by far. The moment he reached his room, he shed his backpack, placing it on the bookshelf beside his drawing table, and picked out one of the neatly stacked cellophane-wrapped sketchbooks from the bottom drawer of his nightstand.

He opened the wrapper carefully so as not to tear it. After each sketch, he would slip the sketchbooks back into the cellophane as an extra measure to protect them from moisture and other elements that could accidentally damage them. He laid the freshly opened book in the center of the drawing table, running his hands across the thick textured paper. His first order of business was creating the title page, which needed to be just as elaborate as every drawing that would eventually be added to the book.

From memory, he first selected the pencil colors that most closely matched the colored scales of the dragon and the moss-covered rocks upon which it was lying. There was no hurry. He'd watched the dragon for several minutes while eating his lunch, and the image was seared indelibly into his memory.

It took him several hours to complete the title page, and once finished . . . it was magnificent, incorporating the dragon's colors as well as elements of its most prominent physical characteristics. Satisfied it was an accurate representation, Jake turned the page and immediately went to work on bringing his first dragon to life inside the pages of the sketchbook.

Jake never made assumptions in his drawings or inferred details that he hadn't actually seen. The drawings were as factual as mathematics, with no allowance for deviation or speculation, yet his clinical accuracy did not detract from the artistic beauty of the images. It enhanced them.

For most people, the image of a dragon is akin to that of a flying dinosaur. This was no dinosaur. It was sleek and sinewy. Even at rest, it exuded a sense of brute strength tempered by grace and elegance. Its markings adapted and changed as quickly as did the shadows created by the sun breaking through the canopy of cedar trees, gently swayed by the afternoon breeze.

By now, Jake was completely immersed in the mental recollection of his dragon. He worked fast not because it was necessary but because he himself was anxious to see the completed depiction of the amazing beast he'd discovered that morning.

With him having been able to observe the dragon inconspicuously for several minutes, most of the details flowed quickly from his mind, through his fingertips, and onto the page by way of his adeptly wielded colored pencils.

The dragon's eyes were an altogether different matter. He'd caught only a fleeting glimpse of them before the dragon had narrowed them into mere slits to avoid detection. For those details, Jake would need to make another visit to the cove, and this time, he would need to get closer.

CHAPTER 3

AFTER JAKE HAD spent hours upstairs in the sanctity of his bedroom, the smell of dinner being prepared by his mother downstairs finally broke through his wall of concentration. The sun was already setting, and Jake's father would be home soon.

"That must be some fish you caught today, Jake," said his mother, smiling toward him as he washed and dried his hands at the kitchen sink.

Nodding silently, Jake went about setting the table for dinner, placing plates in the exact centers of three perfectly aligned place mats on the dining room table. Knives and forks were placed to the right and left sides of the plates, respectively, and drinking glasses were set in the upper right-hand corners of each place setting.

Jake's mother had grown accustomed to his lack of discourse, and although he wasn't one for socializing, he was a very smart and obedient child. He needed only be told once what was expected of him, and after that, you could set your watch by his punctuality in completing his daily chores.

School guidance counselors had labeled him as everything, from mentally challenged and autistic to an emotionally disengaged sociopath. The truth was he was none of those things. Jake's perception of reality was void of subjectivity. He saw and accepted people, places, and things exactly as they appeared to him without making excuses for their shortcomings or buying into the hyperbole they peddled to ingratiate themselves in the eyes of others.

His bluntness was often misconstrued as hostility when, actually, Jake harbored no animosity toward anyone or anything. His purity and honesty were simply relics of an age gone by and were lost on a generation of cyber liars and bullies. He was inextricably bound to the truth, so rather than expressing his actual thoughts to others, he would remain silent to avoid conflicts that only wasted time without ever convincing anyone to change their minds.

By the time Jake's dad had arrived, dinner was ready, and the table was set. He entered the house every day smelling like sweat and oil, so before coming into the dining room, he would change out of his dirty work clothes and wash his hands and face.

Jake's dad had been working as a heavy equipment operator and mechanic since his grandfather opened the business back in 1982. With the exception of the six years he'd spent serving in the military, Jake's dad had never left Tennessee. He preferred the quiet pace of operating and servicing farm equipment to the crushing pressure of getting tanks and armored vehicles back into action after they'd been damaged or disabled by enemy fire and improvised explosive devices in Iraq.

Jake's mom always kissed him when he came back downstairs into the dining room. The kiss always lasted exactly two seconds, and she always delivered it on tiptoe, with her left foot curled behind her.

After Jake's dad blessed the meal, his mom always served them first before preparing her own plate, and no one ate a single bite until she was seated.

Jake noticed all these mini routines and rituals. They provided a sense of normalcy for him, reassuring him that the most important things in his life would always remain constant even in the face of perpetual change.

Jake loved his parents and could always count on their support and understanding. After dinner, Jake sat on the couch with his dad in the living room, sharing the drawing he'd done of that morning's catch. The image was so vividly detailed, it seemed capable of jumping right off the page.

"This is amazing," said Jake's father. "You're such a talented young man."

Jake truly admired his dad, Samuel Earle Payne, or Big Sam, as his friends and customers called him. He stood nearly six feet and eight inches tall in his stocking feet and was a large powerful man.

During his military tour in Iraq, he was awarded the Silver Star Medal for heroism when the vehicle he had been driving encountered an

IED during a routine patrol on the outskirts of Baghdad. The explosion ripped a hole in the right rear quarter panel and flipped the entire vehicle into a ditch on the opposite side of the road. Two of the soldiers riding with him were killed instantly. Two more were pinned beneath the left side of the vehicle, unable to move, as it burst into flames.

Dazed but alert, Samuel was able to free himself from behind the wheel, and as the remaining vehicles in the patrol took up defensive positions, he was able to kick out the windshield and escape across the hood. Ignoring the stinging impact of small arms fire into his right shoulder and buttock, he noticed his brethren in uniform still trapped inside and beneath the overturned vehicle. The other soldiers in the patrol squad were busy engaging the enemy and returning fire, and time was quickly running out.

Placing his feet against the sloped wall of the drainage ditch and his hands inside the frame of the shattered rear passenger window, he was able to lift the vehicle enough for the two pinned men to escape, and despite the heat of the flames drawing nearer, he held it up long enough for his colleagues to recover the bodies of those who'd died inside from the explosion.

When he finally dropped the burning wreck, his clothes were smoldering, and two men from another vehicle were running toward him. As he dragged himself out of the ditch, additional small arms projectiles impacted the back of his flak jacket and his left arm and hand. A moment later, the vehicle exploded behind him, and he lost consciousness, coming to days later aboard a hospital ship in the Persian Gulf. He returned home to a hero's welcome, humbly claiming he'd only done what was necessary. That day, his friends dubbed him Big Sam, and justifiably, the label stuck.

Everyone looked up to Big Sam, but his biggest fan by far was his son. Of the few words spoken by Jake each day, most of them were exchanged with Samuel, who always found time to listen with an open mind.

On weekends, Samuel and Jake would walk down to the lake together, discussing whatever came to mind. Sam would point out the various animals inhabiting the forest, describe the differences among the types of trees, explain which plants were useful and which ones to avoid, and teach Jake the differences among the fish they caught and the techniques applied to catch them. On every trip down to the lake, Sam would emphasize the importance of never leaving anything other than footprints behind.

"Mother Nature does just fine without us," he'd say, "but we'd be lost if she ever turned against us."

At the age of ten, Jake was already an excellent woodsman, using his natural artistic abilities to document the detailed lessons he'd learned from his father.

Closing the sketchbook for the evening, Jake asked his dad, "Is it all right if I ride my bike down to the lake again in the morning?"

"Sure, son," answered Sam. "But stick to the cove and be back by noon so I can see you when I take my lunch break."

"Yes, sir," answered Jake, heading up the stairs. Pausing on the first landing, Jake stopped to ask, "Dad, do you think dragons really exist?"

After taking a moment to consider Jake's question, Sam answered, "I suppose they could. Just because I've never seen one doesn't mean they don't exist."

Smiling and nodding to himself, Jake seemed satisfied by his dad's answer and turned to head upstairs.

"Good night, son," said Sam. "I love you."

"I love you too," replied Jake, closing his bedroom door behind him.

Later that night, when his mother peeked in to pull up his covers and kiss him good night, Jake was sound asleep and smiling.

CHAPTER 4

WHEN A PERSON'S conscious mind is always analyzing, calculating, organizing, and categorizing everything it encounters, once it finally is at rest, the sleep state it falls into is very deep. That, combined with the excitement of an eleven-year-old boy who has just encountered the singularly most amazing find even *his* mind could imagine, provides a highly fertile environment for the most extraordinary of dreams.

On some level, Jake realized he was dreaming. In real life, there was no way he could run that fast or jump that high. He wasn't nearly strong enough to lift the boulder he was holding over his head nor cast it that far out into the sea. *The sea?* How on earth did he even get there?

The scaly body armor he was wearing was flexible yet apparently impenetrable, and it moved with him as if it were his own skin. Perhaps it was. His movements were fluid and gracefully executed with the skill of a master martial artist.

He found himself running toward the edge of a cliff overlooking the tumultuous black waters of an angry sea. Below him, the waves crashed forcefully against the jagged rocks at the base of the cliff. Reaching the edge at full speed, he leapt in a perfect swan dive, disappearing over the edge and out of sight, only to reappear seconds later, sitting astride the back of his magnificent dragon as it soared upward toward a crescent moon in the cold night sky.

The alarm clock on the nightstand beside his bed abruptly ended his nocturnal adventure as reality crept through his bedroom window along with the dark gray morning sky. The memory of the dream faded quickly as Jake dressed, grabbed his backpack, and headed out the back door to his bicycle.

The ride down to the lake was somehow different this time. Everything, even in the predawn semidarkness, seemed to be more vivid, and the entire forest seemed more vibrant and alive than ever before.

He could hear the jingling of the rooster tail lure at the tip of his fishing rod as he peddled down the bumpy dirt road toward the lake, which he could clearly smell. The woody scent of the surrounding red cedar trees felt heavy in the morning air, and even his own heartbeat seemed to echo audibly inside his chest.

When he closed his eyes, he could see himself from a perspective of looking down from above. He quickly opened his eyes and looked upward at the gray morning sky. There was nothing. The pounding of his heart was like a drumline in his own head. It felt as if all his senses were being supercharged by some external force over which he had absolutely no control.

Despite the risk of a serious fall, Jake closed his eyes once again. The vision of himself riding down the road on his bicycle immediately reappeared. This time, Jake kept his eyes tightly shut, navigating the road only from the vision being projected into his mind. Smiling to himself, Jake continued pedaling, his confidence building with each second.

Daring to go even further in this uncanny experiment, Jake let go of the handlebars and extended his arms out to his sides like wings. Skillfully dodging any and all objects and obstacles along the bumpy dirt road, Jake laughed out loud, feeling giddy and invincible.

Suddenly, he noticed something on the road ahead of him, something small but stationary. Zooming in with his extraordinary new vision capability, he noticed it was a small white dog, and it was staring directly at him. The vision was accompanied by a single word, trumpeted loudly into his mind: *Stop!*

Instantly, his eyes flew open, and his hands returned to the handlebars as he locked up the brakes on his bike, sliding to a full stop just inches from the tiny dog sitting defiantly in the middle of the road, staring at him.

Jake's heart was pounding in his chest, and his eyes were now wide open. His hands were shaking, and he was only a breath away from hyperventilating.

The little dog was the polar opposite of Jake, sitting there quietly with the confidence of a . . . dragon.

"Good morning, Jake."

The words formed clearly in Jake's mind as he stared at the little dog in front of him. Looking around as if he were expecting to find someone hiding behind the trees in the thick forest, Jake once again stared at the little dog, whose ego seemed large enough to block the entire road.

"Is this close enough?" asked the voice in his head.

"What?" asked Jake, confused by the question.

"You said you needed to get closer. Is this close enough?" asked the strange voice again.

"I never said that," replied Jake directly to the dog this time.

"Said it, thought it. It's all the same to us now," replied the cocky little dog.

"Actually, I was thinking about something a little bigger than you," replied Jake.

"Close your eyes again, count to three, and then open them slowly," said the dog.

"Why?" asked Jake skeptically.

"You're talking to a Chihuahua in the middle of a dirt road at five thirty in the morning," said the dog. "How much more bizarre could things possibly get?"

This time, Jake did as he was told, slowly closing his eyes as the little Chihuahua gradually faded out of sight behind his eyelids. After counting to three, he slowly opened them. The little dog was gone.

Instead, he stood face-to-face with the creature he'd seen the day before in the shadows of the cedars along the opposite shore of the lake. It was nearly exactly as he'd drawn it in the pages of his sketchbook, but this time, its golden eyes were wide open and trained directly on him.

While the characteristics of the creature's body were familiar from his mental recollection, the eyes were indescribable. They were similar to the eyes of a reptile in that the pupils dilated and constricted vertically; however, that was where the similarities came to a screeching halt. The pupils were surrounded by irises that extended all the way to the edge of the creature's eyes and seemed to be filled with liquid in a continuous boiling motion. It reminded him of how black coffee looked in a cup when cream was being poured into it, except in this case, the cream was made of bright molten gold.

Putting down the kickstand, Jake dismounted his bicycle and slowly walked toward the creature. Cautiously extending his hand, he placed it on the creature's snout.

Visions of the previous night's lucid dream immediately flooded back into his mind in breathtakingly vivid detail. Jake snatched his hand away as if he'd touched a hot stove, stumbling backward and falling to the ground.

"You're a dragon!" exclaimed Jake, his eyes wide in disbelief.

"No, Jake," replied the magnificent creature. "I am *your* dragon."

CHAPTER 5

IT TOOK A moment for Jake to adjust to this new reality in which he was suddenly living. *Dragons* do *exist, they can communicate telepathically, and they are very,* very *large.* His mind was reeling as he considered the implications, which basically extended to infinity.

Slowly walking around the dragon, Jake took in every stunning detail, forcing his mind to accept as fact something that even *he* would previously have dismissed as pure nonsense. Placing his hand against the scaly side of the magnificent beast, he was surprised at the warmth and texture of the scales. Each large scale seemed to be made up of hundreds of smaller overlapping scales. Unlike fish scales, they were soft, pliable, and unexpectedly warm.

Standing close to the dragon was like standing near a fireplace in winter. The heat radiating from within its body was pleasant and welcoming, and even with Jake's hand pressed firmly against its side, the temperature was never uncomfortably hot.

Continuing along the dragon's left flank, Jake was amazed at the intricacy of the scales and how they interlocked, creating an overlapping, seemingly airtight seal. Its hind legs were sinewy and powerful, sloping gracefully downward into massive five-toed webbed feet bearing claws nearly two feet in length. Its tail made up a full third of its total body length and seemed to be somewhat of a counterbalance to the long S-shaped neck and front legs and massive chest and abdominal cavities. The tail culminated in a horizontal webbed fin that collapsed and expanded like a folding handheld fan.

Making his way back up the right side of the dragon, Jake realized its left and right sides were exact mirror images of each other. At the apex of the creature's neck, tucked in behind the jawline, were slotted gills similar to those found in a catfish. The rigid skin covering them was firmer and much tougher than the scales surrounding them.

The dragon's head and face were different from the rest of its body. The skin was leathery and smooth, and the bone structure beneath it was thick and very, very hard. Its eyes were located at the sides of its head, protruding slightly beyond the jawline, allowing it a nearly 360-degree view of its own body. When closed, the dragon's eyes, mouth, nostrils, and gills were completely sealed, and the openings were nearly undetectable.

Traveling the full length of the dragon's body, from the crown of its head and down its spine to the end of the tapered tail, was a continuous, flexible webbed fin, reminiscent of a horse's mane.

Standing in front of the dragon once again, looking deeply into its luminous golden eyes, Jake asked, "How do you fly without wings?"

The dragon extended its legs, standing tall. Along its sides, seams previously undetected by Jake opened up to reveal massive webbed wings unfolding and extending nearly twenty feet in each direction. Observing the dragon in all its glory, Jake was awestruck at the sheer enormity of the creature.

As the dragon retracted its wings, they once again folded in neatly along the sides of its body as the scales surrounding them raised slightly to allow those along the edges of the wings to interlock with them. Amazingly, once retracted, the wings were invisible within seconds, and the seams around them were completely undetectable.

The dragon sat patiently, allowing Jake to inspect it thoroughly without so much as a murmur. It'd been watching the boy for many years, comprehending what no one else around him ever could.

People were reluctant to believe in what they themselves were unable to see. It was easier for them to ostracize the exceptionally gifted and visionaries among them than it was for them to accept that *they* were, in fact, the ones who were lacking.

Dragons could see everything, both in stable and transitional dimensions. For dragons, spirits and living beings were equally real and observable, oftentimes even occupying the same spaces, unaware of each other's presence. Although there were mediums and clairvoyants who could sense the presence of interdimensional beings, dragons could actually see and interact with them . . . and so could Jake.

Jake's ability to traverse this interdimensional rift made him an outcast on both sides of it. Trying to convince a spirit that they'd already left the physical plane of living beings was just as difficult as trying to convince the living of the very existence of spirits. Unable to resolve this ever-present dilemma, Jake found it easier to withdraw from both sides completely, and over the years, he'd become indifferent to the insults and attacks from each of them.

As Jake and his dragon made their way down to the lake, Jake's mind was buzzing with questions that were telepathically answered by the dragon as quickly as he could think of them. He enjoyed interacting with the dragon because he didn't need to speak at all, and his thoughts and questions were understood as clearly as they were answered.

Sensing Jake's extreme comfort with communicating strictly telepathically, the dragon realized the potential danger of enabling him to withdraw even further into himself. As it was, Jake spoke very few words each day, even though, judging by the clarity of his thoughts, his vocabulary was quite extensive and his delivery eloquent.

"You need to speak more often," stated the dragon in a form of telepathy that was perceived by Jake as spoken words despite the fact that the dragon never actually spoke. "I am here to help you become the man you'll need to be to fulfill the destiny that lies before you."

Jake attempted to continue their telepathic exchange; however, the dragon refused to answer, funneling Jake into a spoken conversation.

"Why can't we just continue as we did before?" asked Jake.

"Communication is power, Jake. The more people you can reach with your words, the more effectively you can shape the world around you," answered the dragon.

"But it's so frustrating for me, trying to explain things to people who have no interest in what I have to say," said Jake. "They only want to make fun of me anyway."

"You, Jake, are endowed with gifts and talents few people in history have ever known. There will often be situations in which *you* will need to show humility for the greater good," the dragon replied.

Jake realized the validity of the dragon's words, but he'd never been comfortable enough around anyone other than his parents to let his guard down and actually *be* approachable.

"You don't have to be an expert at it right away. Just show a little interest in others once in a while," added the dragon.

"But how?" asked Jake. "I don't even know where to start."

"Over the past six hours, you've asked me everything about my physical characteristics and abilities yet absolutely nothing, not one single question, about my life on a personal level," stated the dragon. "You have yet to even ask my name."

After carefully considering their extensive, hours-long conversation, Jake once again had to admit the dragon was right. "What *is* your name?" he finally asked.

"I am called T'Aer Bolun Dakkar."

It suddenly dawned on Jake that it was nearly noon, and he'd promised his dad he'd be back by then. Gasping out loud, he said, "I'm going to be late. I promised my father I'd be back by noon, and I'll never make it in time."

For Jake, breaking a promise to his father was the same as lying to him, and in Jake's eyes, that would be unforgivable. Quickly gathering his things, he knew there was no way he'd make it back in time, and he began to panic.

"Calm yourself, Jake," said T'Aer Bolun Dakkar. "I will get you home in time to greet your father."

Rising onto his hind legs, T'Aer Bolun Dakkar expanded his massive wings and wrapped them around Jake, his bicycle, and all the belongings he'd brought with him. There was a sudden rush of wind that lasted only a few seconds. When the wings unfolded again, Jake was standing in his own backyard at the foot of the steps leading up to the back screen door.

"Jake, I can nearly set my watch by your punctuality," said Samuel, opening and holding the door for his son. Looking past Jake into the yard, he asked, "Who's that behind you?"

Quickly turning to look back, eyes wide with anxiety, Jake relaxed when he saw the little white Chihuahua sitting there patiently in the grass behind him.

Phrasing his answer carefully so as not to lie to his father, Jake said, "Ummm . . . He came home with me. Can I keep him?"

Looking over the little dog, Samuel smiled as it curiously tilted its head from side to side. "Someone's bound to be looking for such a cute little fella, but I suppose you can look after him until we find out who he belongs to."

"Great!" exclaimed Jake, shocking his dad with his unexpected excitement.

"What do you call him?" asked Samuel, curious.

"I call him T'Aer . . . I mean, Turbo," said Jake, calling out to him, "Come on, boy!"

Together, the two of them rushed joyfully past Samuel and up the stairs to Jake's room.

CHAPTER 6

AS JAKE AND Turbo sat together in Jake's room, they returned to their telepathic exchange of ideas to avoid arousing the suspicion of Jake's parents. Communicating in total silence, they revealed their histories to each other.

Jake and Turbo were both loners in their own right but for entirely different reasons. Jake avoided people because he found trying to fit in with them annoying. To be accepted by them, he had to pretend he couldn't tell when they were lying and act as if their embellished stories were actually believable.

Many people lied without realizing they were doing so by repeating unsubstantiated stories, never even attempting to verify their authenticity. Others, when asked how they were doing, always responded by saying they were "fine," even when they most definitely were not.

Jake's gut reaction was to always challenge and expose these lies, even when doing so created awkward and embarrassing situations for everyone involved. Although his challenges were always proven to be annoyingly correct, the truth became a liability for him because people were reluctant to talk to or even around him about anything.

On the other hand, T'Aer Bolun Dakkar explained that his avoidance of humans was essential for his survival. For centuries, dragons had been hunted, captured, enslaved, and killed by kings and their armies all over the world. Often they were forced into battle and used as weapons to kill innocent men, women, and children at the direction of a ruthless authoritarian dictator.

The eggs of female dragons were harvested and auctioned off to the highest of bidders among kings, emperors, and pharaohs, who made absolutely sure they were the first humans to see and be seen by the freshly hatched dragons, creating an unbreakable lifetime bond between them.

In centuries past, dragons committed horrible atrocities at the behest of the humans with whom they'd bonded. Their only hope of freedom was for them to outlive those humans, at which point they would be unbound for the remainder of their lives. However, since dragons could live up to three hundred years and even longer if they chose to hibernate for an era, many kings would have them destroyed as they approached the end of their lives to prevent their dragons from turning on the people of their own kingdom after the king's death.

Dragons could survive on any carbon-based diet, but their dietary preference was saltwater fish, for which they would travel a thousand miles or more in a single night to consume. Some would fly from distant mountain and desert regions, while others followed rivers for hundreds of miles to where they met the ocean.

When deprived of access to the oceans, dragons could eat virtually anything, the most dangerous of which were coal and ash. These carbon sources created a type of acidic reflux that was then expelled from them in the form of fire, similar to napalm, a very useful and destructive weapon in the hands of a mad king.

Whether traveling by air or by water, dragons were very stealthy and very fast. With their powerful wings, they could ascend to the outer limits of the atmosphere, where they used the earth's rotation to shorten their flight time to the ocean. In the water, their webbed feet and fanned tails made them the fastest inhabitants in all the seven seas. Their scales adjusted naturally to resist the enormous pressure of even the deepest points of the ocean, becoming more and more rigid as the pressure increased and then relaxing again as they approached the surface and the oceanic pressure decreased. When submerged, the dragons' gills filtered oxygen from the water, allowing them to breathe in much the same manner as fish and other aquatic animals.

Dragons were the only creatures on Earth capable of ascending from the bottom of the Mariana Trench to sea level at full speed and then breaching the surface and taking immediate flight to the upper atmosphere without suffering the devastating effects of rapid decompression. Their extremely high internal body temperature protected them against both the freezing cold of the deep blue sea and the chilling edge of Earth's thin upper atmosphere.

The scaly hide of a dragon was literally impenetrable. It could not be cut, pierced, or incinerated by anything known to man, and it was impervious to caustic and corrosive agents of all kinds. An unbound dragon's only vulnerabilities were its airways via either the mouth, nose, or gills, through which they could be sedated with any number of common tranquilizers; however, to dragons, ingesting oleander leaves in any form was fatal.

Another significant reason for dragons' avoidance of humans was a well-kept secret of kings, emperors, and pharaohs for generations. The blood pulsing through the veins of dragons was of pure molten gold.

When dragons died, their bodies decomposed rapidly. Even the massive bones of their skeletons were quickly reduced to dust and ash. However, their blood seeped deeply into the ground in long narrow veins. For centuries, the blood of dragons was the primary source of a ruler's wealth. It was collected and minted into coins, statues, jewelry, and adornments bearing the likeness of the king.

Unbound dragons sought out the most remote of locations in which to die, hiding and barricading themselves inside remote mountainous caverns, active volcanic fissures, and deep oceanic trenches, which were nearly inaccessible to those who would seek to collect their precious life's blood.

While the golden age of dragons had ended centuries ago, most of the gold left behind by their decomposing carcasses had yet to be discovered. Most likely, it never would be.

As Jake sat quietly, listening to and learning about the history of Turbo's ancestors, at times fascinated and other times horrified, he realized the depth of their connection. Still, there was one question he had yet to ask.

"T'Aer Bolun Dakkar, has anyone else ever seen you?" asked Jake.

"I have seen a multitude of humans over the past century," answered the dragon. "You are the first who has ever seen me."

Gripping his chest just below the heart, the dragon forcefully removed a single scale. Unlike those of a fish, a dragon's scales did not regenerate, and the hole in its impenetrable armor would now be forever its only other vulnerability.

"Close your eyes and place your hand here, Jake," stated the dragon.

Jake did as he was instructed without questioning its purpose. Closing his eyes and placing his hand over the hole left by the missing scale, he felt a surge of warmth pass through his entire body. As he held his hand in place, the dragon pressed the scale he'd removed against Jake's chest, directly over his heart.

The intense burning sensation was accompanied by the smell of seared flesh as the scale molded into Jake's chest and disappeared without a trace. The heat from the dragon's chest traveled quickly through Jake's hand and up his arm and spread throughout his entire body. Jake was shaking in the chair where he sat across from the dragon, but his mind was clear as if detached from the spectacle entirely. He watched from the dragon's perspective as T'Aer Bolun Dakkar laid him gently on the bed and covered him with the blanket.

Later that evening, when Jake's mother peeked in to tell him dinner would be ready in an hour, she smiled as she saw Jake lying on the bed, with the little white Chihuahua curled up next to him.

Both were sleeping peacefully.

CHAPTER 7

JAKE AWAKENED IN time to make his way downstairs, wash his hands, and set the table for dinner before his father arrived. As his mother was preparing a salad on the countertop, Jake approached her from behind, wrapping his arms around her waist and hugging her tightly.

"I love you, Mom," he said, to her complete astonishment.

Shocked, she quickly turned and bent down to hug Jake tightly to her, kissing his forehead.

"Why are you crying, Mom?" asked Jake, noticing the tears running down her cheeks.

"Because I love you too, Jake," she replied, smiling at him and caressing his face. The smile continued as she released Jake from her embrace and turned to finish preparing the salad at the counter.

Sarah loved Jake more than anything on Earth and was the first to defend him against the insinuations made by lazy guidance counselors and teachers who would rather medicate a child into tranquility than rise to the challenge of actually listening to him.

Jake knew more than any of the educators entrusted with the responsibility of teaching him. His ability to quickly comprehend complex intellectual and mathematical theories and then to correctly apply them was baffling. So often, he'd been accused of cheating when the simple truth was he devoured knowledge as if it were the only nourishment capable of sustaining him, and he remembered everything.

For Jake's teachers, it was impossible for them to capture and hold his attention for any extended period. By the time they'd finished explaining step one, Jake had already correctly executed step ten and withdrawn into the secrecy of his ever-present sketchbooks. Although to them, he appeared not to be paying attention, he would ace every pop quiz, daily test, and major exam without even the slightest of errors.

For Sarah, Jake was an angel. The precise and caring manner with which he treated everything entrusted to him was beautiful to her. He was thoughtful and kind, treasuring even the simplest of gifts and never asking for anything more than he was given.

Jake and Sarah heard Sam's truck pulling into the garage just as dinner was ready.

As Sam came through the door, he called out, "Jake, can you give me a hand here, son?"

Jake rushed to the door to find his dad holding a large bag of dog food, food and water bowls, a doggy bed, a collar and leash, and several colorful balls in various sizes.

"Wow!" said Jake, genuinely excited. "Thank you, Dad."

As Sam headed upstairs to wash up before dinner, Jake placed the bag of food on the bottom shelf of the cupboard closest to the back door and the doggy bed and bowls in the corner next to his seat at the dining room table.

Without a second thought, Turbo made himself comfortable in the doggy bed, while Jake filled his bowls with food and water. When Sam entered the dining room, Sarah kissed him as she always did, and the three of them sat down at the table, where Sam blessed the meal. Sarah prepared plates for Sam, Jake, and herself, and once she was seated, everyone, including Turbo, ate.

After dinner, Jake helped Sarah clear the dishes from the table and load them into the dishwasher before retiring to the living room with his father.

"How was your fishing trip this morning, son? Did you catch anything other than Turbo?" asked Sam, smiling.

"No, sir. Turbo was pretty much it," replied Jake with a grin. "But I did sketch some nice pictures of him," he said, handing his sketchbook to his dad.

Flipping it open, Sam was shocked at the clarity of the first image, looking back and forth between the dog sitting on the floor near Jake's feet and the detailed sketch he held in his hands. The resemblance was stunningly accurate down to the last whisker.

With Jake's fishing and wildlife sketches, he didn't have the actual subjects of the pictures readily at hand. This sketch was different. The emotional impact of it could be felt physically. It was almost as if Turbo had shaped himself to mirror the sketch rather than the image capturing the likeness of *him*.

The most riveting aspects of the sketch were the eyes. They seemed to be alive in the image, with Turbo's gaze following Sam regardless of the angle or position in which he held the sketch. Lowering the sketch to look directly at the little dog again, Sam felt as if both of them were scrutinizing him under their watchful gazes.

"This is remarkable, Jake," said Samuel, looking at his son, who was confidently smiling up at him.

"Thank you, Dad," said Jake, feeling more confident than he'd ever felt in his entire life.

As Sam was flipping through the remaining sketches in the book, each image was as breathtaking as the first one, seeming to possess a life of its own as it languished within the pages of Jake's sketchbook.

Handing the sketchbook back to Jake, Sam said, "I am very proud of you, son. I've always been proud of you, but even so, I never realized just how talented you really are."

Jake was smiling ear to ear as he closed the sketchbook and slipped it back into the cellophane wrapper before heading up the stairs to his bedroom, with Turbo right on his heels. At the first landing, he stopped, looking back at Samuel.

"Dad, you are my hero, and I love you very much," said Jake in the most serious tone Samuel had ever heard from him.

Beaming, Samuel replied, "I love you too, son. Good night."

"Good night, Dad," responded Jake as he and Turbo disappeared into his bedroom, closing the door behind them.

After cleaning and putting away everything in the kitchen, Sarah joined Sam on the couch in the living room, curling up next to him the way she had years ago, when they were still dating.

"Jake did the most wonderful thing today," said Sarah, explaining what had transpired in the kitchen earlier that evening. "Somehow that little dog brings out a beautiful type of confidence in him."

"I totally agree," said Sam. "Perhaps we should have adopted a dog for him sooner."

"No . . ." responded Sarah. "It's not *a* dog. It's *that* dog. There is something special about him that Jake connects with and relates to. Earlier this afternoon, I peeked in on them while they were napping upstairs. That little dog is already so attached to Jake and is never more than an arm's length away from him. He gives Jake a sense of confident calm I have never seen in him before."

Nodding, Sam said, "Well, whatever their connection, it seems to benefit both of them, and I'm all for it. I just hope no one shows up to claim that little dog after Jake has become so attached to him."

"Who around here would have a Chihuahua anyway?" asked Sarah. "And who in their right mind wouldn't be turning Wilson County upside down to find him if he'd strayed off and gotten lost?"

"Well," said Sam, "we'll just have to take it day by day and see what happens. In the meantime, Jake and Turbo are both happy together, and that is a blessing in and of itself."

Together, they sat on the couch, lost in their own thoughts, feeling more relieved and enlightened than they had in a very long time. They both loved Jake with all their hearts, and his happiness was paramount to them. If that little Chihuahua could bring about such a wonderful change in their son, then it was their hope that he would remain with them forever.

CHAPTER 8

THAT NIGHT, AFTER Jake's parents had retired to their bedroom and were sleeping deeply, T'Aer Bolun Dakkar nudged Jake, who was also sound asleep.

Through groggy eyes, Jake sat up, asking, "What is it?"

"I need to go out," said the dragon. "As delicious as the food your father brought home for me is, I need to eat something more substantial."

Sliding into his house slippers beside the bed, Jake quietly crept down the stairs with Turbo and let him out into the backyard.

Through the screen door, he asked, "How long will you be gone?"

"We," responded the dragon. "You're coming with me."

"What?" responded Jake, suddenly wide awake. "I can't go out this late at night. My parents will be very upset with me if they notice I've left the house at this hour without their permission."

"We are bonded now, Jake," explained T'Aer Bolun Dakkar. "I need to feed on fish, and I can no longer travel that far without you."

"But the lake is less than two miles from here," Jake said. "You can be there within a few seconds, and I'll just wait here to let you in when you get back."

"We're not going to the lake," said the dragon. "We're going to the ocean."

"*What?*" responded Jake. "The ocean! *Which ocean?*"

"There are storms in the gulf tonight, so fishing there would be less productive. The Atlantic is the most logical choice. It's closer, and the skies are clear. Feeding there would be our best option for tonight if we leave right now," stated T'Aer Bolun Dakkar matter-of-factly.

"Right now?" asked Jake in disbelief, looking around nervously. "I'm wearing pajamas and slippers, and I'm not even sure I *have* anything warm enough to fly in. The Atlantic . . . *Are you out of your mind?*" Jake ranted in a loud whisper so as not to wake his parents.

"Calm yourself, Jake," replied T'Aer Bolun Dakkar. "As am I, so too are you."

Unveiling himself from the disguise of a little dog, the dragon assumed his full form right before Jake's astonished eyes. Reaching out, he touched Jake's shoulder with a single razor-sharp talon. The sensation spreading quickly throughout Jake's body was similar to the feeling of submerging oneself into the warm water of a bathtub. It was wonderful.

Stepping back, Jake looked down at his feet, which were now covered in dark flexible scales. Excitedly lifting his pajama top, he noticed his hands, along with the rest of his body, were covered in the same impenetrable armor. His fear was gone, wholly replaced by the irresistible urge to fly.

Fully expanding his wings, T'Aer Bolun Dakkar lowered the left one to the ground. Shedding his pajamas and grabbing onto T'Aer Bolun Dakkar, Jake swung easily onto the dragon's back as if he'd done so a thousand times before. Seated comfortably above and slightly in front of the point where the dragon's wings met his torso, Jake pressed his legs firmly against T'Aer Bolun Dakkar's sides.

The dragon's scales instantaneously melded with those of Jake's body armor, yet they did not hinder Jake's movements in any way whatsoever. When he moved, the scales released and reconnected in a nanosecond. As long as any part of Jake's armor was touching any part of the dragon, the connection was inseverable unless Jake willed it to be so.

"Are you ready, Jake?" asked the dragon.

"Yes!" exclaimed Jake in great anticipation.

Using his powerful hind legs and feet, T'Aer Bolun Dakkar leapt upward. Even without employing his wings, they were easily launched five hundred feet into the air.

Spreading his wings while still on an upward trajectory, T'Aer Bolun Dakkar began flapping them, scooping up massive amounts of air and propelling the two of them higher and higher with each undulating motion. Within seconds, they'd already reached an altitude at which Jake could clearly see the curvature of the earth below.

"This is amazing!" screamed Jake into the wind at the top of his lungs.

"There's no need to yell, Jake. Our thoughts are bonded as tightly as our body armor," the dragon explained.

"I know!" said Jake, continuing to scream out loud. "But this is so amazing!"

Suddenly, the lights of the Eastern Continental United States gave way to the complete and utter blackness of the Atlantic Ocean. Even from their dizzying altitude, the dragon—and thereby Jake—could easily recognize the huge swarming bait ball of Atlantic herring boiling a hundred feet beneath the surface of the ocean.

Retracting his wings and diving, the dragon rapidly descended through the night sky and into the cold black water, leaving barely a ripple in the waves surrounding it. The scaly body armor of both Jake and the dragon fully absorbed the kinetic energy of the impact as they pierced the surface, slipping through it like an eel.

Spiraling downward into the icy depths, the corkscrew-shaped path was marked by the oxygen escaping from beneath the dragon's scales as they dove deeper. Instinctively, Jake was holding his breath, waiting for them to surface so that he could refill his lungs with oxygen.

"There's no need to hold your breath, Jake. As long as we're connected, I can breathe for both of us," his dragon explained.

Sure enough, Jake relaxed to realize his mouth and nose were sealed, and the oxygen filtered from the water by the dragon's gills was being directly infused into his own lungs through his body armor.

Underwater, Jake assumed a different riding position, placing his hands on either side of the dragon's neck. With his feet trailing behind him, he was able to glide through the water, anticipating and mimicking every move the dragon made instantaneously.

Time and again, they skirted the outer edges of the bait ball as T'Aer Bolun Dakkar fed on the herring swarm from different vectors of attack with each subsequent pass. Within minutes, he'd consumed the entire school of them.

From the deep black soul of the ocean, the dragon headed upward, his webbed feet and tail displacing massive amounts of water as they rocketed toward the surface. Breaching the oceanic skin, they were two hundred feet above the water before the dragon deployed his wings, beating the air to submission as they flew higher and higher. The view was breathtaking as they headed north toward the aurora borealis, with Jake clinging tightly to the dragon's neck and sides.

"Let go, Jake," said the dragon. "Let go and jump!"

Blindly trusting T'Aer Bolun Dakkar, Jake did what he'd been longing to do since they'd slipped the surly bonds of Earth. He jumped with his arms outstretched. The sensation of weightlessness was exhilarating. At that altitude, he was able to glide at such a gradual slope, he was certain he could've remained airborne for an hour or longer.

Dipping his left wing and spiraling downward, T'Aer Bolun Dakkar matched Jake's glide path, coming up beneath him, catching him in midair. As they were powering up into the dark sky once again, Jake released himself at the apex of the climb, which catapulted him upward toward the outer edge of the earth's gravitational pull. Dangling there between Earth's atmosphere and outer space, Jake and his dragon floated gracefully in the void, surrounded by billions of magnificent stars.

After several minutes of blissful observation, T'Aer Bolun Dakkar said, "It's time we headed back," breaking the fragile silence of the moment.

Nodding, Jake swung astride the dragon, and they started their glide path back down to Earth. As they shed altitude, the sun began to appear on the curved horizon to the east and would soon be illuminating the sky above Tennessee. A few minutes later, they were landing quietly in Jake's backyard.

Slipping into his pajamas, Jake reluctantly climbed the stairs to the back porch, the scaly body armor disappearing into his skin without a trace. As he stepped inside through the back door, Samuel was just walking into the kitchen to start a pot of coffee.

"What are you doing outside at this hour, son?" asked Sam.

Once again, carefully selecting his words so as not to lie to his father, Jake said, "Turbo needed to go outside to take care of his business."

A few seconds later, the little white Chihuahua trotted up the stairs, through the back door, and into the kitchen, where he stopped at Jake's feet.

"Are you two going fishing down at the cove today?" asked Samuel.

"Not today," said Jake. "I think I'd like to sleep in for a while this morning."

"Then I guess I'll see you this afternoon for lunch," replied Sam as Jake and Turbo headed out of the kitchen toward the stairs.

"Have a nice day at work, Dad," said Jake, grabbing ahold of the bannister and heading up the stairs. "We'll see you this afternoon."

At the top of the stairs, Jake and Turbo disappeared into Jake's bedroom, climbing back into bed. Jake was asleep before his head could even hit the pillow.

CHAPTER 9

FORTUNATELY FOR JAKE, dragons didn't need to eat two tons of fish every single night, so planning their midnight seafood excursions was somewhat manageable. On the other hand, Jake had never felt anything as exhilarating as flying with T'Aer Bolun Dakkar, and he cherished every opportunity to do so.

For dragons, flying through the night sky and feeding on North Atlantic herring was an essential yet mundane occurrence for them. Although having Jake as a wild card allowed T'Aer Bolun Dakkar to see it from a fresh perspective, the activity itself was something he'd been doing for well over a century. What he *did* find new and exciting was being a dog.

When T'Aer Bolun Dakkar had first encountered Jake at the fishing cove, he instinctively scanned the young boy's thoughts, searching for an unintimidating form to assume for their first face-to-face encounter. He had discovered that Jake liked dogs but was somewhat wary of larger ones. The form he had chosen was literally taken from the fragment of a fast food commercial still embedded in Jake's long-term memory.

T'Aer Bolun Dakkar knew relatively little about dogs and had never really understood the connection between humans and canines. Of course, he'd interacted with dogs over his hundred-year history. Most of the time, they were mastiffs and wolfhounds used by huntsmen to locate dragons who'd outlived the humans with whom they'd previously bonded.

T'Aer Bolun Dakkar's mother had been such a dragon. After seventy years of loyal service to Queen Victoria, she was released from her bond by the queen in 1900 after having mated with an Egyptian dragon king. Shortly before her death in 1901, the queen issued a royal mandate ordering the unconditional release and nonpursuit of her dragon, a female fire drake named Sahar Talin Dakkar; however, there were spies within the royal cabinet who betrayed her trust and, upon her death, sought to recapture the dragon and steal her eggs.

Having uncovered this conspiracy before the traitors could enact their plan, Sahar Talin Dakkar escaped to Iceland, where she laid and protected her three perfect eggs. Only weeks before they were due to hatch, her lair was discovered by dragoneers who'd been dispatched throughout Northern Europe and Scandinavia with their mastiffs and wolfhounds in search of Sahar Talin Dakkar and her coveted eggs. Upon returning from the icy North Atlantic, where she'd been feeding, she discovered that two of the eggs had been removed and had been loaded onto an armada of ships anchored at the base of the craggy cliffs below her hideout.

Her rage was immeasurable, dwarfed only by the horror of knowing her young were in danger, hidden aboard one of the many ships below, which were weighing anchor, preparing to leave the remote harbor. Not knowing which of the ships were carrying the precious cargo, she took the remaining egg and hid it in the mouth of an active volcanic fissure on the northernmost point of the continent. The intense heat of the surrounding lava would prevent both the dragoneers and their dogs from even getting close to the egg while having absolutely no negative effect on the unborn dragon within. After securing the egg, Sahar Talin Dakkar feasted, gorging herself on the hardened lava at the edge of the flow, its high carbon content feeding the acidic reaction within her upper digestive tract.

Leaving the area of the active volcano, Sahar Talin Dakkar set out on her mission to rescue her unborn babies. She quickly caught up to the ships bringing up the rear of the armada, unleashing her wrath upon them. The effect of her unbridled fury was devastating, melting the steel vaults surrounding the munitions aboard the ships. They exploded violently in the face of the unrelenting heat generated by the dragon's flaming breath. The bodies of the mercenaries aboard the ships were instantly vaporized as Sahar Talin Dakkar attacked ship after ship, annihilating over half of the fleet before the carbon fueling her fiery regurgitations was depleted.

Continuing her relentless attack with her razor-sharp talons, she ripped into the decks of the ships, grasping and capsizing them while being ceaselessly pelted by the barrage of artillery rounds pounding into the impenetrable scales of her dragon hide. Within minutes, eight of the twelve ships had been completely destroyed and were well on their way down to Davy Jones's locker.

Diving into the freezing-cold water beneath the remnants of the armada, Sahar Talin Dakkar sank her talons into the hull of one of the remaining ships and, leaving her wings deployed, dragged the entire vessel with its crew to the bottom of the sea. Ascending rapidly, she crashed into the bottom of the lead vessel, with the thick bone structure of her forehead acting as a battering ram. The ship was broken in half, with the bodies of the crew flying into the air like lifeless ragdolls.

Of the two ships remaining, only one of them engaged the dragon, releasing a barrage of artillery fire in her direction, while the other ship attempted to flee across the vast ocean with nowhere to hide. Dropping lower and flying mere feet above the water's surface, Sahar Talin Dakkar used the edge of her wing to slice into the steel hull of the ship engaging her, eviscerating it at the water line. It sank quickly, joining the rest of the woefully inadequate armada beneath the icy black water of the North Atlantic.

Hovering above the final ship, she finally saw her missing eggs. They were suspended in a massive tank filled with water steeped in oleander oil. Atop the tank were dragoneers with harpoon guns poised to pierce the thin shells that were the only barrier between her offspring and the deadly concoction surrounding them.

As the ship's captain looked across the surface of an empty ocean that had borne one of Europe's deadliest fleets mere minutes prior, the full realization of his failed mission sank in. Taking one final look upward at the impending doom hovering above his ship, a crooked grin crossed his lips as he gave the order.

"Fire!"

Sahar Talin Dakkar's heart sank with grief as the harpoons pierced the eggshells, allowing the poisonous oleander oil to enter the tender airways of her defenseless babies. They were dead within seconds.

Sahar Talin Dakkar was heartbroken as she felt the fragile connection to her young being permanently severed at the hands of this greedy, inhumane monster. Swooping down to the deck, she snatched up the captain with one of her hind feet, sinking a claw into his lower back, deftly severing his spinal cord while leaving him alive to witness her maternal rampage.

While he watched, she used her deadly wings to decapitate the mercenaries who'd manned the harpoon guns, along with everyone else who had dared to remain on deck. Gripping the port-side railing of the ship with her other hind foot, she lifted the ship into the air as bodies and unsecured cargo slid downward to the lower side of the dangling ship before crashing through the railing and into the sea. Carrying the ship high into the air, Sahar Talin Dakkar released it, watching it turn to rubble as it smashed against the surface of the unforgiving ocean.

She would not give this captain the honor of going down with his ship. Instead, she ascended high into the air, flying back to the northern coast of Iceland, where she slowly lowered him into the lava of the active volcano. His screams were music to her ears as his body was slowly consumed and then swallowed completely by the liquid hell.

Realizing her Icelandic lair was no longer safe, she retrieved her remaining egg, carrying it deep into the Yukon–Koyukuk region of Alaska, where she remained with it until T'Aer Bolun Dakkar finally slipped from his shell and was able to fend for and defend himself.

During Sahar Talin Dakkar's battle with the dragoneers' armada, she'd been severely wounded, having sustained a direct hit below her heart where the bonding scale for Queen Victoria had been removed. Although with the help of her sole offspring, T'Aer Bolun Dakkar, she persisted for another twenty-five years before finally succumbing to the injury, she still expired centuries before her time.

Dragons passed their knowledge on to their offspring through both genetic coding and telepathic communication. In this manner, nature could guarantee that the history of a dragon's mother was passed on to her offspring. The father's DNA, although a major contributor to a dragon's strength and physical attributes, was not a part of the genetic memory coding, which was solely transferable from female dragons.

While T'Aer Bolun Dakkar was genetically programmed to know everything about his lineage and the capabilities and limitations of being a dragon, being a Chihuahua was a totally different matter, a matter that he was surprisingly curious to learn as much about as possible.

CHAPTER 10

AS TURBO, T'AER Bolun Dakkar could move freely among humans without stoking fear or anxiety in them. Surprisingly, his tiny teacup-sized proportions made him anything but inconspicuous. It was impossible for him to accompany Jake anywhere without drawing an extraordinary amount of attention.

Although Turbo was undoubtedly the intended recipient of the fawning attention from absolute strangers, Jake was the one forced to interact with them. After all, no one was crazy enough to believe a dog could answer all the questions they hurled at him with their hyper-sweet soprano voices. Women seemed especially vulnerable to Turbo's vexing charm.

"Oh my god!" they would say. "He is so cute!"

Most often, that was followed by them kneeling and extending the backs of their hands as a gesture indicating they weren't a threat to him. Of course, they weren't a threat. He was a dragon, for heaven's sake. Nevertheless, Turbo would go along with them, accepting their overt capitulation in the presence of his apparent greatness.

As dragons, T'Aer Bolun Dakkar's ancestors commanded respect by their sheer daunting presence, by far the largest and most dangerous animals on the planet; no one even questioned their physical superiority. Conversely, Turbo could circumvent the emotional barricades erected by total strangers simply by tilting his little head first to one side and then the other while looking at them.

While T'Aer Bolun Dakkar was still a fledgling, his mother taught him about her lineage and the royal traditions that had been an ever-present part of her service to Queen Victoria. The pomp and circumstance surrounding the queen was always precisely scripted, down to the choreographed trot of the horses pulling the royal carriage. Sahar Talin Dakkar had, of course, been one of those noble mares. As a part of the team pulling the carriage, she could remain close to the queen when traveling outside the secure palace grounds and offer a level of security her royal protection squad could not. The royal trot was a hallmark of the queen's equestrian team and drilled into them for hours on end until it became their natural gait. Sahar Talin Dakkar watched the team closely and was able to precisely mimic their movements, naturally fitting in with them.

Drawing on his mother's memories, T'Aer Bolun Dakkar utilized this gait while accompanying Jake as Turbo. It never failed to capture the attention of even the most distracted eye as he pranced about like a royal stallion at a hefty four and a half pounds.

Contrary to popular belief and medieval folklore, dragons did not growl or roar. Except for the flapping of their powerful wings or heavy footfalls while walking, they were nearly silent, communicating their words and thoughts telepathically. For this very reason, it was difficult for T'Aer Bolun Dakkar to do the one thing dogs were known for—barking. When he did bark, the whimsical sound created by his miniature vocal cords was anything but threatening, invoking more smiles and laughter than fear in those on the receiving end of it.

The unique combination of the head tilting, the royal trot, and the whimsical bark were apparently the most potent aphrodisiac on the planet because *everyone* loved Turbo.

By extension, Jake was forced to engage with nearly everyone they encountered. He now walked with his head up and shoulders back, and watching everyone smile at Turbo made Jake smile back at them.

In the local park they frequented together, Turbo would playfully engage with other dogs and finally realized what those various-sized colorful balls were for. He watched, mesmerized, as a young girl about Jake's age took a fuzzy green ball and tossed it into the field as far as she could. The Irish setter accompanying her took off like a shot, chasing the ball down and catching it in midair after the first bounce. Joyfully dashing back across the field with the ball in his mouth, he obediently dropped it at the girl's feet, excitedly wagging his tail in anticipation of her next toss.

Turbo was watching too, and when the girl tossed the ball again, both the setter *and* Turbo simultaneously took off in hot pursuit of it. The sight of the large dog dashing across the field, with Turbo bounding along behind him, was nothing short of hilarious. At times, Turbo would disappear completely in the tall green grass, only to bound above it again, even closer to the setter than he had been before. Vanishing one final time into the sea of green, this time, Turbo reemerged ahead of the Irish setter, with the fuzzy green tennis ball in his mouth.

The ball was so large compared to Turbo that he was only able to grasp it by sinking his teeth into the fuzzy felt covering. Dashing back to the young girl, he passed by the setter, who seemed perplexed not only that Turbo had beaten him to the ball but also that he was already headed back across the field with it.

The humor of the situation was completely lost on Turbo, who was prancing in place, waiting for the ball to be thrown again. The setter found nothing funny about it at all and was aggressively rushing across the field toward Turbo with a serious bone to pick. He was about ten paces away on a collision course when Turbo sensed the negative energy emanating from him. He turned to directly face the approaching setter but did not back down even a single step. Suddenly, it was as if something had drained the fight completely out of the dog bounding toward him, and he came to a dead stop mere inches away from the tiny white Chihuahua. There was no barking or growling by either dog as they stood there, nose to nose, staring at each other.

What there was remained unseen by everyone except for the Irish setter, who was suddenly seeing the reality of his precarious situation. Making eye contact with a dragon, even one posing as a Chihuahua, was chilling. Whether you were human or canine, standing face-to-face with the most dangerous creature on Earth was sobering, to say the very least.

The setter ceded his claim to alpha status instantly, assuming a docile posture toward Turbo so as to not even give the appearance of provocation. At the same time, Turbo showed unexpected grace toward the setter, choosing not to belittle him in front of his human or the other dogs observing the confrontation from a distance.

Instead, the two of them bounded off *together* after the tennis ball, thrown again by the young girl. This time, Turbo allowed the setter to win by a length so as not to make it obvious he was holding back. The confrontation between the two of them was over from that point forward. There would be no grudges held or unspoken schemes to "get even" as both the setter and Turbo returned happily to their humans.

Jake, who had observed the entire episode from an elevated perspective, understood exactly what had transpired between Turbo and the setter. Realizing that even in the form of a Chihuahua, T'Aer Bolun Dakkar still possessed all the strength and ferocity of a full-sized dragon, he was curious as to why he hadn't chosen to "teach the other dog a lesson."

T'Aer Bolun Dakkar said to Jake, "Humiliating someone, anyone, for anything creates a new enemy for you. By allowing your ego to dictate your actions, you alienate others by forcing them to fear your physical and/or intellectual superiority rather than view it as something from which they can also benefit."

After giving Jake a moment to fully digest his statement, he continued, "Jake, even when you are 100 percent certain that you are correct, it is always worth it to leave room for enlightenment or even an epiphany. By allowing others to perceive the truth in their own minds, you offer them a means of retaining their honor, which is not possible if you humiliate them into submission."

"But sometimes people say things that are just utterly wrong," said Jake. "Why should it even be necessary for me to entertain their obvious errors?"

"Because when someone else is wrong, even utterly wrong, their lack of knowledge is not a liability for you. However, if you can leave the bread crumbs that allow them to discover the truth for themselves, you positively motivate them, thereby creating a desire in them to discover the truth in all things," replied T'Aer Bolun Dakkar, "and the truth is an asset that benefits all of mankind."

Jake nodded in understanding, considering all the times he'd missed such opportunities and vowing to show more compassion and understanding in future confrontations.

In the meantime, it had been three days since T'Aer Bolun Dakkar and Jake had visited the ocean to feed, and tonight they were visiting the Pacific. As soon as Samuel and Sarah were sleeping deeply, Jake and T'Aer Bolun Dakkar were airborne, heading west.

CHAPTER 11

ALL YOUNG BOYS dreamt of flying at some point in their lives, and tonight Jake was once again living the dream. In the few days following Jake's bonding with T'Aer Bolun Dakkar, his eyes had been opened to a whole new world of possibilities and actual experiences.

Because of their bond, the two of them were in a constant state of information exchange, providing Jake with the seemingly endless fountain of knowledge he'd so desperately wished for and T'Aer Bolun Dakkar with real-time insight about the species that had influenced the most consequential evolutionary changes on the planet.

While in flight, Jake could see these changes and compare them to the visual references locked into T'Aer Bolun Dakkar's genetically coded memories. In fact, detailed maps of the entire earth were a part of that genetic coding, making it impossible for a dragon to ever become lost or disoriented. Furthermore, dragons could literally *see* jet streams and were able to correctly predict the weather *everywhere* days in advance. For T'Aer Bolun Dakkar, there was no such thing as a weather prediction. He simply stated what the weather would be, and it was so.

At one point in history, there had been too many dragons inhabiting the earth. Instinctively, they reduced their own numbers to avoid overplundering the oceans of fish and damaging the earth's delicate ecosystem. Men, on the other hand, had no such insight nor the self-discipline to reign themselves in when it came to protecting the environment for their future generations.

Over the centuries, dragons had watched as humans exhausted the planet's resources, pushed entire species into extinction, released toxins into the air that were dangerous to their *own* species, and turned a blind eye to the obvious damage they'd done to the earth's atmosphere, all because of their insatiable greed for wealth.

It was easy to be indifferent to these changes when you were only reading about them in history books and science journals. From a dragon's perspective, high above the earth, looking down on what *was* and being able to compare it to what *had been* as little as fifty years ago, the differences were sobering.

Nevertheless, Jake's view while astride T'Aer Bolun Dakkar was nothing short of breathtaking and humbling. That big blue marble down there was home to over seven billion people, yet from this altitude, not a single one of them could be seen. However, the Great Pacific Garbage Patch created by their waste and lack of regard for Mother Nature could be.

The words of Jake's father rang clearly in his mind: "Leave nothing behind but footprints."

"Your father is a good and wise man, Jake," said T'Aer Bolun Dakkar. "The world would do well to have more men like him."

Jake smiled to himself, drawing parallels between Big Sam and T'Aer Bolun Dakkar. Both were strong, brave individuals willing to sacrifice themselves for the betterment of everyone. They both stood on the principles of fairness and honor and were committed to making the right decision, even when it wasn't the easy one.

The steep banking maneuver gave notice that T'Aer Bolun Dakkar was preparing to dive toward the huge swarming bait ball of Pacific herring just beneath the surface of the water below them. In mid-descent, he suddenly pulled up, taking on altitude once again.

"What's the matter?" asked Jake, confused at the dragon's abrupt course alteration.

"Patience, young Jake," replied T'Aer Bolun Dakkar while continuing to tightly circle the area above the submerged bait ball from a higher altitude. A few seconds later, he said, "There."

Looking down, Jake saw a second dragon approaching from the north and then diving into the water to feed on the teeming bait ball. The dragon was easily twice the size of T'Aer Bolun Dakkar.

"*Who is that?*" asked Jake excitedly.

"That is Tao Min Xiong," explained T'Aer Bolun Dakkar. "He is the eldest of all dragons and the genetic origin of many of us."

"How old is he?" asked Jake.

"He's over a thousand years old and is revered by all dragons," replied T'Aer Bolun Dakkar. "Most dragons have never seen him, and only a very few ever will."

"Wow!" exclaimed Jake, staring down in disbelief. "Have you ever seen him before?"

"No," replied T'Aer Bolun Dakkar. "This is the closest I have ever been to him."

The two of them observed from above as the massive dragon devoured the bait ball and ascended to the surface, where he deployed his enormous wings and headed north. After watching him disappear into the darkness, Jake and T'Aer Bolun Dakkar remained silent for several minutes, letting the significance of this experience sink in.

Heading south, they soon discovered another bait ball teeming below the surface. Without a splash, they entered the water like a spear, corralling and feeding on the tightly grouped school of Pacific herring until T'Aer Bolun Dakkar had consumed it completely.

As they were exiting the water, the starlit sky above welcomed them once again into its vast embrace. Heading east, they crossed into North America over the pristine coastline of British Columbia, and in what seemed to be only a few minutes, they were descending into the familiar surroundings of Jake's backyard.

Upstairs in Jake's bedroom, Jake asked T'Aer Bolun Dakkar, "Do dragons ever socialize with one another?"

"Associations among dragons are very rare occurrences," answered T'Aer Bolun Dakkar. "Even after mating, the male and female dragons part immediately, with both returning to their own roosts, having no further contact to each other."

"So do the female dragons raise the babies alone?" asked Jake. "Do the offspring ever get to meet their fathers?"

"Yes and no," replied T'Aer Bolun Dakkar. "Raising the young is the sole responsibility of the female, and it's a responsibility she would *never* surrender to the male under *any* circumstances. Female dragons are ferocious guardians of their young and would erase an entire bloodline to protect them if necessary. The knowledge of our fathers is passed on to us through the genetic coding of our mothers. All male dragons actually become their fathers, while female dragons become their mothers. An Egyptian fire drake male who breeds with a Northern European Jormungand female will produce male fire drake offspring and Jormungand female offspring, yet all the dragon whelps will inherit the genetically coded memories of the female, which include her memories of the male. In this way, every species of dragon is essentially preserved, even if the low number of male or female dragons in certain regions makes it impossible to find an exact species match."

"How many dragons are there?" asked Jake.

"Centuries ago, our numbers were such that we could blacken the sky, blotting out the sun over an entire kingdom under the umbrella of our wings," explained T'Aer Bolun Dakkar. "However, as the human population increased, the resources we required to survive became more and more scarce, and dragons were blamed for everything, from droughts brought on by overfarming the land to plagues that arose from the unclean conditions in which humans chose to live.

"We were hunted relentlessly and killed by the tens of thousands. Our food and water supplies were poisoned, forcing us to retreat into the farthest reaches of the earth to avoid the comingling of humans and dragons. Through genetic adaptation, many of us were able to develop camouflage and concealment capabilities that allowed us to hide our very existence from humans. Still, our numbers continued to decrease until we were forced to the edge of extinction by greedy dragoneers, who sought to rid the earth of the dragon scourge while lining their pockets with the solidified blood of our brothers and sisters.

"Tao Min Xiong is a dragon king, revered as the grandmaster of all dragons as it was he who had developed the telepathic techniques that allowed dragons to manipulate the trans-dimensional rift. Using his genetic hereditary knowledge, dragons can shapeshift and appear in an altered form in this dimension while simultaneously occupying the same space as a dragon in an unseen parallel dimension. Today there are fewer than three hundred dragons left on Earth. However, because of our unique means of preserving our genetic integrity, all twenty species of dragons continue to persist, even as our numbers decrease."

Realizing Jake had already dozed off and was sleeping soundly, Turbo curled up next to him, saying, "Good night, Jake. May *our* bond last forever."

Together, they slept.

CHAPTER 12

IT WAS AMAZING how quickly a summer break could come to an end and even more amazing how much a person could mature during that short period. The insecure, withdrawn little eleven-year-old boy had evolved into a self-confident twelve-year-old young man.

Not only had Jake's teachers noticed the difference, but also, his classmates recognized it. Students expecting to confront a timid little recluse with a total absence of social skills suddenly found themselves dwarfed by Jake's intellect. Not only was he willing to voice his thoughts, but also, he was able to do so authoritatively while retaining an objective, nonconfrontational air about himself.

Furthermore, once having dreaded physical education activities because of his total lack of hand–eye coordination and general clumsiness, Jake had completely blossomed over the course of the summer break. He was now quick, agile, and unexpectedly strong for a boy of his age. In addition to catlike reflexes, he was also fast, easily outrunning boys who were both older and larger than he was.

He'd still dive into his ever-present sketchbooks whenever possible, but he was no longer shy about putting his artwork on display. The images he could capture with a dozen colored pencils were more vivid and captivating than the sum of all selfies taken by his classmates over the course of the entire summer. In short, Jake had gone into the summer as a nondescript caterpillar and returned as a monarch butterfly.

While T'Aer Bolun Dakkar had never accompanied Jake into the school, he was always nearby, and their mental connection was constant and uninterrupted. Big Sam's agricultural supply warehouse was within walking distance of the school, so Jake and Turbo would ride to work with Samuel on weekday mornings, where Turbo would "stay" with Jake's dad during the day. After school, Jake would finish his homework assignments in Sam's office and then tidy up around the shop, making sure the shelves were stocked and the floors were swept clean before they closed up the store and headed home.

Jake would also observe how skillfully Sam could repair anything, whether it required replacing worn-out items or fabricating parts for aging farm equipment when replacement parts were no longer available. Sam never sent a customer away without a solution and a repair they could depend on.

When it came to equipment repairs, Big Sam was a household name throughout Middle Tennessee. His custom fabrications were often the difference between farmers getting their crops to the market or having them rot in the fields. Although Sam was well aware of the integral role his skills played in the success of many of the state's farmers and agricultural entities, his prices were always fair, and his terms were flexible enough to allow his customers to pay after their harvest had been brought to the market and sold.

Had it not been for Big Sam, several of the state's independent produce and dairy farmers would have been pushed out of business years ago. Even as things now stood, large agricultural corporations were ceaseless in their efforts to make farming more difficult and less lucrative for local family-owned farms and businesses. Samuel's resourcefulness and willingness to work with local farmers was an integral element in keeping local farms in business and the greedy farming corporations at bay, something that had not gone unnoticed by them.

Over the past few years, one company in particular had been buying up farmland at every opportunity. The Middle Tennessee Agricultural Corporation—or MTAC—arrived on the scene and immediately began hiring up all the laborers in the region, making it difficult for small family-owned farms to find the workers they needed during harvest season. Furthermore, they were paying their workers an hourly rate, which was much too high for private farmers to match. The result left family-owned farms with ripe produce in the fields and no means of harvesting it.

At the last minute, MTAC would sweep in with a lowball offer to buy the produce at a rate that, although humiliating, was the only solution left for the farmers. Afterward, MTAC would descend on the farms with a crew of a hundred or more laborers, some of whom had worked those very same farms in previous years. They'd pick the fields clean within a single day, taking the produce directly to the processing and distribution centers, where they were paid the full market price after having borne none of the costs for planting and growing it. As a massive corporation, they could easily absorb the cost of the overpaid labor with the profit they generated from swindling hardworking farmers out of their harvest.

On the other side of the coin, by saturating the market with produce, they effectively drove down the prices processing plants and distribution centers were willing to pay, making it tough for noncorporate farms to cover their costs and remain above water. Their multipronged assault forced family-owned farms to the verge of bankruptcy, at which point they had no choice but to sell, and of course, MTAC was there with another humiliating offer.

One by one, the family-owned farms, even those dating back several generations, were forced out of business, leaving MTAC to fill the void they'd masterfully orchestrated. With profit margins as tight as they'd become, Big Sam was often the saving grace for that handful of private farmers who chose to persist despite the best efforts of MTAC to torpedo their businesses.

Samuel was well aware of MTAC's efforts to surveil his business. They'd stop by his store in their brand-new pickup trucks, walking through the aisles as if looking for something specific yet leaving with a BearClaw and an RC Cola. They'd tried to usurp Big Sam's employees on numerous occasions, failing to recognize the sense of loyalty shared by his small but talented crew.

All of Big Sam's employees were military veterans. A few of them had served with him in Iraq, while others were from different branches of the military. They'd routinely rag on one another using nicknames. Former airmen were "wing nuts," naval seamen were "swabbies," marines were "leathernecks," and army soldiers like Big Sam were "grunts." Despite their service rivalries, first and foremost, they were brothers and treated one another as such.

With skills that came from years of military service under the most extreme of conditions, they were able to find solutions for nearly any problem, and obstacles were simply minor bumps along the superhighway of experience shared among them.

That kind of loyalty wasn't a commodity that could be bought and sold, and Sam's willingness to hire them when others wouldn't even give them a chance had earned him a level of respect no amount of money could ever undermine. He'd given them a chance to earn an honorable living and stood by them even in the toughest of times. They would most certainly stand by Big Sam, come what may.

Sam and Jake were always the last to leave the store. Signing off the security checklists posted near every exit of the building, Sam would always make certain everything was in "military order" before setting the security alarm and online surveillance systems prior to leaving the property.

On the way home, Jake would listen attentively to his dad's account of the day, remembering even the most unremarkable details of the conversation. By the time they had reached the house, dinner was always ready, and Jake would fill Turbo's bowls, wash his hands, and set the table, while Sam washed up and changed his clothes upstairs. The kiss on tiptoe, the blessing of the meal, and Sarah preparing everyone's plate before taking her seat at the table remained the closing act of each busy day.

Even after a century of experience navigating the outermost reaches of the earth, T'Aer Bolun Dakkar found this to be one of the most beautiful experiences he'd ever been part of, and like Jake, he felt a sense of belonging he'd never known before. After only six months as Turbo, T'Aer Bolun Dakkar discovered something with this family that had eluded him for over a hundred years: love.

CHAPTER 13

SAMUEL ENJOYED HAVING Turbo around while Jake was in school. When he was a young boy working for his father, they had a shop dog named Farmer. All he ever did was lie around the shop, but everyone who came through the door more than once remembered him. He was a very friendly German shepherd, but his size was a great deterrent to would-be shoplifters.

Turbo was completely different. He followed Sam around the shop as if he were keeping an eye on everyone and everything. Although he was never in the way, he was always right there whenever Sam would turn around looking for him. He was also very clever, seeming to know in advance when Sam needed a shop towel, a screwdriver, his cell phone, or other small items around the shop, and would bring them to Sam, often before he could even ask for them. While it was obvious Turbo was Jake's dog, he seemed to care about everyone who touched Jake's life in any possible way.

For a dragon who'd spent the majority of his life in solitude or lurking in the shadows to avoid contact with humans, T'Aer Bolun Dakkar felt surprisingly at ease with them as Turbo. Their world was much different from the genetic memories passed on to him from his mother. While there were still and would probably always be humans around the planet locked in eternal conflicts over imaginary lines drawn on paper depictions of the real world, here in Jake's Tennessee, those problems seemed to be a galaxy away.

For centuries, dragons had been the ultimate weapon for royal armies, tilting the advantage decidedly in their favor on battlefields while securing their kingdoms as the ultimate deterrent against aggression.

As mankind's standoff weaponry became more and more advanced, the military superiority formerly guaranteed by dragons was all but erased. The final blow came on August 6, 1945, when a manmade flying machine dropped a relatively small balloon-shaped object over

Hiroshima, one of two top-secret locations housing Emperor Hirohito's dragon squadrons. Three days later, a second one fell over Nagasaki.

Mankind had finally discovered a weapon capable of generating the heat necessary to kill a dragon. Within four days, Emperor Hirohito's entire dragon force had been decimated, along with over two hundred thousand of his people.

Having dragons suddenly presented an unheard-of danger to those kingdoms harboring them. The undiluted fear of being targeted with such horrific weapons of war led rulers around the globe to destroy them by the thousands. Those that had survived scattered into the most desolate locations on Earth, severing and avoiding all contact with humans.

Dragons were never intended to be used as weapons. Their nature was similar to that of their distant genetic cousin, the blue whale. They could have coexisted with humans and never presented a danger or threat to them. Only through human intervention were these peaceful giants bred and taught to kill, something no dragon would ever choose to do if given a different option.

While T'Aer Bolun Dakkar was absolutely nonviolent by nature, he was genetically programmed to protect Jake, with whom he had bonded, and Jake's territorial surroundings. Anyone and anything important to Jake was also important to T'Aer Bolun Dakkar.

Big Sam's store hours of operation developed organically over the years. Monday through Thursday, he was open from 7:00 a.m. until 5:00 p.m. because that was when his farming clients were most likely to need him. On Fridays, he'd close up shop at noon, releasing his staff and taking care of his online orders and office documentation until Jake showed up after school at 3:30 p.m.

That Friday, shortly after 1:00 p.m., while Sam and Turbo were alone in the store, Sam received a call from Sarah. She told him that the principal, Mr. Edwards, had called from the school and informed her that Jake had been injured in shop class. She said the injury wasn't serious, but it would probably be best if Sam could pick him up and take him to see a doctor.

Without a word, Sam grabbed his keys and darted out the door. Looking at Turbo, he said, "Hold the fort down, Turbo. I'll be back with Jake in a few minutes."

He locked the door behind him, leaving Turbo alone in the store. Although this did seem unusual to T'Aer Bolun Dakkar, Sam would often drop everything to help out clients who were unable to make it to the store because of an emergency.

Being in constant contact with Jake, Turbo knew everything was fine as far as Jake was concerned; however, not having heard Sam's conversation with Sarah, he was unaware of the principal's claim. Not worried, Turbo sat there in the store, looking out the glass front door, awaiting the return of Sam and Jake.

Sam parked in the school parking lot about the same time the white MTAC pickup truck pulled into the gas station across the street from Big Sam's store. As Sam trotted up to the main entrance of the school, Turbo sat up, watching the suspicious stranger crossing the street and disappearing around the corner, down the side of the store.

In the principal's office, Sam was met with curiosity by Mr. Edwards, who had no idea what Sam was talking about and most definitely had not called Sarah. Using the classroom intercom, the principal called the shop class teacher, asking him to release Jake and send him to the main office to meet his dad.

At the store, Turbo followed the sound of the stranger's footsteps in the gravel alongside the store. They stopped outside the side door near the back of the building. T'Aer Bolun Dakkar was already sending this information to Jake, who was running up the long corridor from the classroom toward the front office, where his dad was waiting.

The muffled sound of the window in the side door breaking clearly signaled the intentions of whoever it was outside the store. Telepathically, T'Aer Bolun Dakkar told Jake he should hurry as he rushed into the principal's office.

"Are you all right, son?" asked Sam, confused by the entire situation. "Were you injured in class today?"

With a quizzical look on his face, Mr. Edwards asked, "What's going on here, Jake? Your dad said your mom called him about some sort of injury. Is something wrong?"

Ignoring the principal completely, Jake looked frantically into his father's eyes, saying, "Dad, we have to go! We have to go right now!"

"Sure, son. We're going right now," said Sam, leaving the office with Jake, to the total bewilderment of the principal, as they hurried outside to Sam's truck.

Being born of fire, T'Aer Bolun Dakkar instinctively recognized the smell of accelerants. He watched the gloved hand reaching in and unlocking the door through the broken window, and as the intruder stepped inside and closed the door behind him, Turbo made his stand.

Inside Sam's truck, Jake told his dad, "You've got to hurry, Dad! Someone's breaking into the store!"

"*What?*" replied Sam, stepping on the gas. "Are you sure about that?"

"Yes, sir," replied Jake, carefully choosing his words. "I got a message from someone telling me they saw it happening."

They were still a couple of minutes away as Turbo stood inside the doorway, with the intruder turning to face him. Seeing the little Chihuahua there, baring his teeth and growling at him, elicited no more than a chuckle. Turbo's whimsical little bark caused him to laugh out loud as he pulled the lighter fluid and matches out of his coat pockets.

"You gonna bite me, little guy?" asked the unwitting intruder, chuckling as he bent down, reaching a hand out toward Turbo.

Sam saw the MTAC pickup truck parked across the street just as he was pulling into the driveway, asking Jake, "Where are they?"

"Around the side!" answered Jake.

Jumping out of the truck and yelling back to Jake, "Call 911!" Sam bolted around the side of the building.

He was only a few steps away when the intruder's body came crashing through the door in a hail of splinters and shattering glass. Sam stopped short, instinctively crossing his arms in front of his eyes as if shielding his face from an explosion. Lowering his arms, he saw the man lying there on the ground with the bottle of lighter fluid still clutched tightly in his hand. He was battered and groaning, but he looked none worse for wear.

As Sam approached the hole in the wall where the door used to be, he peered in cautiously through the opening. Inside, Turbo was sitting there as if waiting for a ride at the bus stop amid the contents of the matchbox scattered across the floor. Upon seeing Sam in the doorway, Turbo trotted nonchalantly up to him, looking back down the side of the building where Jake was approaching.

In the background, the sound of sirens filled the air, and onlookers were starting to gather out in front of the store. Moments later, sheriff vehicles were flooding the parking lot, having received several calls from concerned neighbors, including the gas station attendant where the MTAC truck had parked across the street.

Samuel was backing away from the man on the ground with his hands in the air as deputies swarmed the area with weapons drawn. The groggy man lying on the ground opened his eyes to a sea of badges and blue uniforms before being read his Miranda rights and escorted to the back seat of one of the sheriff vehicles in the parking lot.

As the flurry of activity faded and the crime scene was secured, Sam walked through the store with two of the sheriff's deputies, taking a visual inventory of the damage. Other than the broken side door, nothing was missing. In fact, it seemed the intruder hadn't even made it beyond the threshold of the side door before somehow being ejected from the building. Hopefully, a review of Sam's surveillance recordings would bring clarity to what had actually transpired.

Sarah had come to the store a few minutes after the suspect was arrested, picking up Jake and Turbo and bringing them home. All of Big Sam's employees showed up at the store upon hearing what had happened, and after boarding up the broken doorway and resetting the surveillance and security systems, everyone finally headed home after a very long day.

When Samuel came in through the garage door, dinner was ready, and the table was set. After changing out of his work attire and washing his face and hands, he joined everyone in the dining room. That night, the kiss was a bit longer than usual, accompanied by a lingering hug, and Sam's blessing of the meal included additional thanks to God for protecting their family, friends, and livelihood.

After dinner, Jake helped his mom clear the dining room table before retiring to the living room with his dad. There were no sketches to discuss, and the events of the day were still being digested by everyone. After a few minutes, Jake said good night to his dad, and he and Turbo headed up the stairs.

Stopping at the first landing, Jake looked back, saying, "Dad, thank you for believing me."

Pausing for a moment, Sam said, "You saved our store today, Jake. Thank you."

Heading up the remaining stairs, Jake and Turbo disappeared into their bedroom. The ocean would have to wait until tomorrow night.

CHAPTER 14

JAKE AND T'AER Bolun Dakkar lay awake for quite a while that night, considering the events that had transpired earlier in the day. It was obvious someone had lured Sam away from the store so they could vandalize it.

The staged call from Jake's principal was the ham-handed action of a coward who obviously didn't want to face Big Sam, although it had actually worked. Sam left the store immediately after Sarah's call, and had it not been for the connection between Jake and T'Aer Bolun Dakkar, the intruder would have had plenty of time to trash the store and slip away without being discovered.

What would be a bit harder to explain is how a four-pound Chihuahua was able to toss a two-hundred-pound man through a wooden door. Jake had witnessed the entire episode through Turbo's eyes and already knew what the surveillance cameras would have captured.

As the intruder bent down and extended his hand, Turbo seized the moment and lunged upward, ramming his head into the man's chest. The only problem was that he'd overestimated the amount of force it would take to knock the intruder off balance and give Sam time to reach the side door and confront him. Instead, he'd delivered the headbutt with enough force to send the man crashing through the door and out into the gravel, taking part of the doorjamb with him.

"Did you have to hit him so hard?" asked Jake. "You were only supposed to knock him down. Dad could have handled the rest."

"I was unaware of his frailty," replied T'Aer Bolun Dakkar. "I've never faced a human opponent, and I expected him to be sturdier."

"Sturdier?" asked Jake. "You nearly took out the entire wall!"

"I shall make note of that for future reference," replied T'Aer Bolun Dakkar.

"What are we going to do about the video?" asked Jake. "Dad's store is covered front to back and at every entry point. There's no way that wasn't captured."

"But what did they capture?" asked T'Aer Bolun Dakkar. "What *you* saw is not what everyone else will see, Jake. I have dwelled undetected in the presence of kings and walked unnoticed through crowds of thousands. When I do not wish to be seen, I will not be seen."

"I hope you're right about that," said Jake. "Otherwise, we will have a lot of explaining to do, and under no circumstances will I lie to my dad."

"Nor would I ever ask you to," replied T'Aer Bolun Dakkar. "Sleep, young Jake. Tomorrow is a new day and a new beginning."

Surprisingly, Jake slept peacefully through the night, awakening refreshed and anxious to go to the store with his dad. After a hearty breakfast, Sam, Jake, and Turbo headed out, waving to Sarah as they drove down the driveway to the main road.

On weekends, the store was only open from 7:00 a.m. to noon, mainly so customers could pick up equipment that had been repaired or supplies they needed to cover the weekend. When they arrived, Jet and Baker were already inside, turning on lights, opening up the service bay doors, and brewing the military-grade coffee only *they* could drink without diluting it with creamer or hot water.

"Morning, boys!" said Sam, walking in through the front door, with Jake and Turbo in tow.

"Morning, boss!" came their simultaneous reply.

Chuckling as he walked toward Big Sam, Jet asked, "Any surprises in store for today?"

"Only if you want to see the dumbest criminal ever," replied Sam.

"Oh yeah!" said Jet as he and Baker headed into Sam's office.

The look Jake shot at Turbo was one of shock and curiosity as Turbo curled up on the floor next to Jake's chair.

The safest place to keep surveillance footage was at a geographically separate location, so Sam kept everything on the private server at his house. After Jake and Turbo had turned in for the night, Sam and Sarah pulled up the footage to send to the sheriff's office. Reviewing it, they couldn't help but laugh.

As Jet, Baker, and Jake gathered around Sam, he started the video playback. The front-of-house camera clearly showed the man parking the pickup across the street at the gas station and dashing across the road toward the store. The overcoat he was wearing was certainly not appropriate for the seasonably warm weather.

The exterior rear-corner camera captured him walking down the side of the store to the door through which he'd entered. Next to the door, he pulled gloves from his pocket and put them on before breaking one of the windows with his elbow.

The interior front-of-store camera showed Turbo lying on the rug by the front door. His ears perked up as he watched the man approaching the store, heading toward the left side of the building. The camera showed Turbo heading down the hallway as the intruder made his way toward the side door. Surprisingly, Turbo was matching his pace, walking side by side with him, separated by the outer wall. As they reached the back of the building, the rear-interior camera picked up Turbo exiting the hallway, still matching the pace of the man on the other side of the wall. When the man stopped outside next to the door, so did Turbo.

Turbo was sitting there quietly, tilting his head from side to side as the man broke the window, reaching inside to unlock the door. After he entered and closed the door behind him, his head snapped around quickly as he turned to find Turbo standing there, apparently growling at him. Smiling at the sight with his back to the door, he advanced toward Turbo.

Turbo was now barking at him as he reached into his coat pocket and pulled out a box of matches and the bottle of lighter fluid. Laughing out loud, he hadn't even noticed the penlight falling from his pocket and rolling onto the floor behind him.

As he knelt down, reaching out his hand, Turbo lunged at him, headbutting him in the chest. Obviously not prepared for Turbo's bold attack, the man tried to stand up but stepped back onto the tail of his own oversized coat.

While the man was stumbling backward and trying to regain his balance, his heel came down on the tube-shaped penlight, which had been silently rolling back toward the door behind him. Flailing about with nothing to grab onto, he fell backward forcefully into the door, crashing through it just as Sam was approaching from the outside.

The rear-interior camera caught Sam cautiously peeking in through the busted doorjamb as Turbo proudly trotted up to him and exited through the opening as if nothing unusual had happened. By the end of the video, Jet and Baker were laughing so hard, they could hardly breathe. Sam was laughing and banging his hand on the desk.

"I've watched this a hundred times already, and it still cracks me up every single time!" said Sam, trying to catch his breath.

"Play it again!" cried Baker, holding his belly with one hand and wiping the tears of laughter from his eyes with the other.

By now, Jake was laughing too, and even through his tear-blurred vision, Sam realized it was the first time he'd seen Jake actually laughing out loud since he was a toddler.

Sam played the recording over and over, even creating an animated GIF of Turbo's headbutt and posting it on one of his social media pages.

As far as the sheriff's office was concerned, the video provided solid proof of breaking and entering. The man's face could be seen from several different angles, and the timestamps on each of the four camera feeds in which he had appeared were conclusive evidence of what had transpired. Even so, the sheriff's deputies were no less amused than Big Sam and his crew, watching that section of the video dozens of times to belly-aching laughter while gathered around the sheriff's computer monitor.

Later that afternoon, after closing up and securing the store, Jet and Baker headed home as Sam, Jake, and Turbo piled into Sam's truck.

"Jake, that Turbo is something else," said Sam, his cheeks and belly still aching from the sustained laughter of the past few hours.

Jake, grinning from ear to ear, said, "Yeah, there's a lot more to him than meets the eye."

"You're right about that!" exclaimed Sam, barely suppressing the urge to laugh out loud again.

In Jake's mind, T'Aer Bolun Dakkar told him, "Jake, you'll have to tell me more about this 'laughter' phenomenon. It creates such a marvelous aura around everyone. I've never seen anything like it."

"I'll tell you more about it on our trip to the ocean later," said Jake before asking, "Where are we going tonight, anyway?"

"The Indian Ocean is perfect this time of year," said T'Aer Bolun Dakkar.

"Wonderful," answered Jake with a smile as he stared thoughtlessly out the window at the deep green beauty of the rural countryside.

CHAPTER 15

SATURDAY NIGHT WAS movie night in the Payne household. Sam would order pizza or a large bucket of chicken with all the sides, and they'd sit together in the living room, watching movies. Most of the time, they'd watch either something funny or an action-packed thriller. After the movie, Sarah would clear away the leftovers, and by ten o'clock, everyone would be in bed.

At midnight, Jake and Turbo quietly crept down the stairs while Sam and Sarah slept soundly. Lifting off with barely a sound, T'Aer Bolun Dakkar ascended into the night sky with Jake, leaving the tranquility of the backyard far, far behind them.

Jake was always amazed at the altitude and speed of their travel, crossing continents as if they were only tiny puddles of light, quickly flashing into and out of sight as T'Aer Bolun Dakkar sliced through the night sky with his powerful wings. In the time it took for Jake to ride his bicycle down to the lake, he and T'Aer Bolun Dakkar were already crossing over Europe into the Middle East, with the Indian Ocean looming large before them.

T'Aer Bolun Dakkar could hone in on herring swarms from the outer edge of the atmosphere even in near total darkness. Spiraling downward into the Indian Ocean, they glided effortlessly through the water, herding the fish into a giant teeming ball. The speed at which T'Aer Bolun Dakkar could devour such a massive swarm of a million fish or more was astonishing, and after only a few seconds, they exited the water skyward.

"I've been contemplating the theory of laughter," stated T'Aer Bolun Dakkar. "Although I do admit the aura of those who are laughing is very bright and delightful, it seems to me that it came at the expense of another person who didn't fare so well."

"Humor is a peculiar thing," replied Jake. "Often it depends on the viewer's perspective and their opinion of what is funny. Some people will laugh at anything, while others have absolutely no sense of humor."

"In your father's office, it seemed everyone present found humor in the intruder's misfortune. What was their point of agreement?" asked T'Aer Bolun Dakkar.

"That, my friend, is called irony," stated Jake. "When misdeeds intended to harm someone else end up backfiring and the perpetrator becomes the victim, it's the irony of the situation that people find funny."

"I understand," said T'Aer Bolun Dakkar, "but would the perpetrator find humor in that situation also?"

"In the situation, possibly. However, being knocked through a door out into the gravel is difficult to find humorous when you're on the receiving end of it," replied Jake. "Of course, had they seen it from our perspective, it might have been even funnier."

"Should I have not altered the environment from the camera's perspective?" asked T'Aer Bolun Dakkar.

"I'm certainly glad you did," replied Jake. "The irony of a criminal stumbling over his own coattail is easier to explain than the physical impossibility of a four-pound Chihuahua sending a two-hundred-pound man flying ten feet through the air, taking out the entire door and part of the wall before crashing to the ground six feet outside the building."

"Indeed," replied T'Aer Bolun Dakkar.

"Did you actually say you thought he'd be 'sturdier'?" asked Jake, recalling T'Aer Bolun Dakkar's explanation with a chuckle and then a laugh.

"Yes. He wasn't sturdy at all. Not even a little bit," replied the dragon, also feeling Jake's urge to laugh.

As T'Aer Bolun Dakkar was tapping into the emotions exchanged between the two of them, the dragon's body began to rhythmically quake while he recalled the look on the man's face as he went sailing backward toward the door. T'Aer Bolun Dakkar was laughing.

In the dark silence of the earth's upper atmosphere, the two of them were laughing uncontrollably as T'Aer Bolun Dakkar looped and spiraled while convulsions of laughter rippled through his body in waves.

Suddenly, something amazing happened. The dragon's scales opened up like vents, and as the heated oxygen beneath them escaped into the upper atmosphere, he began to glow. The glow continued as he and Jake plummeted through the night sky like meteors, laughing all the way down into the storm clouds gathering over the Southeastern United States. After landing silently in the backyard, they sat together on the back porch looking out into the darkness.

"That was awesome!" said Jake. "I didn't know you could do that."

"Nor did I," explained T'Aer Bolun Dakkar.

As the two of them returned to Jake's room and climbed back into bed, T'Aer Bolun Dakkar said, "Thank you, Jake, for sharing 'laughter' with me."

"You're welcome," replied Jake, adding, "Thank you for sharing the whole world with me."

As the thunderstorm rolled into the county, sending fingers of lightning across the sky, the rain falling gently against the window was the lullaby to which Jake and Turbo slept.

CHAPTER 16

THERE WERE FEW things as peaceful and purifying as a steady rain. The clouds rolling in from the east were dark and heavy with it as they unloaded their cargo of precipitation all over Wilson, Sumner, and Davidson Counties.

While lightning bolts zigzagged across the sky and thunder shook the ground, Jake and Turbo slept peacefully through the night. This was unusual for Jake's parents, who'd never seen him make it through such a storm without a major panic attack.

As Sarah peeked into Jake's room, she saw that he was sleeping like a baby, with Turbo curled up at the foot of the bed. Turbo awakened as she opened the door, and for a moment, she could have sworn his eyes were glowing before he closed them and went back to sleep, curling up next to Jake's feet. She quietly closed the door behind her before going back to bed.

"Is everything all right?" asked Sam as she came back into the bedroom.

"He's out like a light," replied Sarah. "It's like he can't even tell there's a storm going on outside."

"He's got his living security blanket with him, and Turbo seems to keep him calm through everything," said Samuel, smiling.

"Have you ever looked into his eyes?" asked Sarah. "It's almost like he can read your mind. As quietly as I opened the door, he seemed to know I was coming and was looking right at me when I peeked in on them."

"Have you ever looked at his ears?" replied Sam. "He could hear the sun setting with those things. He was probably onto you the minute your feet hit the floor."

"You're probably right," said Sarah, "but his eyes are so beautiful. Not quite green but not really amber either."

"Golden," said Samuel. "They're golden, and yes, I have noticed them. It's kind of hard to miss them, but I don't think he's trying to use mind control on us, and I'm pretty sure he didn't get to choose his own eye color either."

"Of course not," replied Sarah. "It's just that he's the size of a rabbit, with the confidence of a lion. I think *that* is what's rubbing off on Jake. He sees that the size of the outer shell has nothing to do with the man inside of it."

"Exactly," said Samuel. "I was a scrawny kid when I was thirteen and had no idea that five years later, I'd outgrow all my friends. Even so, it took me years to get over the insecurities of being picked on as a kid. Watching the surveillance footage from the other day showed all of us something. From the second that guy showed up at the store, Turbo was ready to take him on to protect the place. He wasn't even a little bit scared while he was shadowing the guy, listening to him through the wall. Then at the back door, as small as he is, he didn't hesitate for a second. He took the fight to that guy and won."

"Like I said, he's an amazing little dog," said Sarah.

Outside, the rain continued pelting the house as it fell in sheets, with no sign of it letting up anytime soon. Jake and Turbo came down the stairs to the smell of fresh coffee and biscuits, joining Sam and Sarah at the dining room table.

"That's some storm outside," said Sam, looking outside through the window.

"It sure is," said Jake. "We saw it coming in last night on the way in."

"On the way in?" asked Sam.

"From the backyard," said Jake quickly. "Turbo had to do his business last night, and we saw the storm clouds headed this way."

"I'm surprised you could sleep through all that thunder and lightning. You used to be scared of storms," said Sarah.

"I was, but then I read that the chance of getting struck by lightning in your entire lifetime is only one in three thousand, and that's if you're outside. Indoors, the chance is even smaller, so I figured the odds were in my favor. Dad says, 'Worrying about something doesn't help. It only makes you feel bad while you wait.' So I decided not to worry," said Jake to the smiles of Sam and Sarah.

Later that morning, Jake sat at the window upstairs, sketching the landscape outside from his bedroom. The brunt of the thunderstorm had passed, replaced by the gentle but steady rain that continued to fall across Middle Tennessee.

Abruptly, T'Aer Bolun Dakkar sat up on the bed, facing the window. "Dragoneers," he said, bereft of all emotion.

Looking out of the window, Jake saw the bland gray sedan coming into view approaching and then turning into the lane leading up to the house. "Really?" asked Jake. "I thought they were something from centuries ago."

"As long as there are dragons, there will be dragoneers," replied T'Aer Bolun Dakkar. "Their greed and thirst for power are unquenchable, and the drive to pursue dragons is a part of their lineage, going back to the days of the great crusades."

"Do they know about you?" asked Jake.

"Know about me? No," replied T'Aer Bolun Dakkar. "But they are very skilled at following up on even the slightest of clues. Something has caused them to follow their bread crumbs to your house."

Thinking for a moment, his eyes widening suddenly, Jake said, "The GIF! That little video clip Dad posted on social media!"

Using his tablet, Jake logged into his own account and then clicked on the link to his dad's profile. Samuel didn't post things very often, so the video of Turbo headbutting the intruder was still at the top of the page. It had been viewed over ten thousand times in the past two days.

"We may have a slight problem," said Jake. "Dad's video has gone viral. It's been viewed all over the world since he posted it. Can they see what *really* happened?"

"No. But they will follow up on anything that appears to be out of the ordinary," replied T'Aer Bolun Dakkar.

Scrolling down through the comments, Jake found one that had generated quite a discussion. One of the deputies who'd arrested the intruder said he'd claimed the video was a fake because he didn't slip and fall like it had shown in the recording. He stated that when the little dog rammed him, it felt as if he'd been hit by a truck. He said the impact sent him flying through the air and crashing through the door and that he hadn't slipped on anything.

The subcomments were mostly critical of the intruder for breaking into the building, claiming crooks would say anything to avoid going to jail. However, one person in the comment thread seemed a bit too interested in the intruder's recollection of the event, asking where it had occurred and who the store belonged to. After finding out the name of Big Sam's business, he suddenly vanished from the comment thread.

Downstairs, the doorbell rang. Jake opened the bedroom door to cautiously peek downstairs as his dad opened the door.

"Can I help you?" asked Sam, suspiciously looking over the strange man at the door.

"My name is Svend Erickson," replied the man at the door. "I'm with the *Nashville Inquirer*, and I wanted to follow up on the human interest aspect of the event that had recently occurred at your store."

Sam might have lived in the country, but he was certainly no country bumpkin. He'd seen so many forms of deception while stationed in Iraq, he could smell something fishy from a mile away. The key to getting the truth was to never let on that you suspected anything. The less information you gave, the more questions they'd need to ask, and with each question, they'd reveal more of what *they* knew. This man, Svend, was definitely not from Nashville or anywhere else in Tennessee. After just a short time in Tennessee, the accent rubbed off on you, and Svend's accent was arguably not even American.

"Well, what y'all wanna know 'bout my store, Mr. Erickson? There really ain't much human interest in a little family business like mine. Farmers 'round here need stuff, so I sell stuff. Their stuff breaks, so when it does, I fix it. Ain't much more to it than that," said Sam in an exaggerated Southern accent.

"I hear your establishment was recently broken into," said the man.

"I'm not sure I'd call it a break-in," replied Sam. "The only breakin' he did was to my door. He didn't even make it inside."

"I hear you have a little hero who assisted you in repelling the intruder," stated the man.

"Nope," replied Sam. "The dang fella was so clumsy, he threw his own self out."

"Might I come inside and have a look at the dog personally?" asked Mr. Erickson. "I'd like to take some photographs for our magazine, and I'm willing to reward you handsomely for the opportunity," he added, reaching into his pocket and withdrawing a tightly bound roll of hundred-dollar bills.

Dropping the feigned accent, Sam said, "Listen, Mr. Erickson, if that really is your name. Let me make this perfectly clear to you. No, you may not come inside. No, you may not see the dog. No, you may not take pictures of anyone or anything inside this house, and you can take your Judas Iscariot reward money and stuff it back into your pocket."

"I'm sorry, Mr. Payne, but—" started the man before being cut off in midsentence.

"My property line starts back at the gate you came through in your rental car," interjected Sam. "Being that it is Sunday, I'm going to be very hospitable and allow you to leave under your own power. Now that offer expires in ninety seconds, at which time you will be leaving under *my* power."

Tipping his hat and retreating down the front porch steps, the man said, "Good day, Mr. Payne. I apologize for having disturbed your Sunday afternoon."

Before getting into his car, he paused to look up at Jake's bedroom window, where he and Turbo had been quietly observing him. Smiling, he got into the car and drove slowly back down the lane. One minute later, he was gone.

"He'll be back," stated T'Aer Bolun Dakkar matter-of-factly. "Dragoneers are as persistent as they are annoying, so I'm sure he'll keep nosing around until he finds something, either real or imagined."

"What can we do?" asked Jake nervously.

"We have one advantage he does not," stated T'Aer Bolun Dakkar.

"And what is that?" asked Jake.

"He only suspects that I am here, and he's never seen me in my natural state," said T'Aer Bolun Dakkar. "We, on the other hand, know exactly who he is and what he looks like, and with your eidetic imagery and artistic skills, you can make his very presence here quite uncomfortable. The last thing dragoneers want is to be exposed to public scrutiny."

Without a second thought, Jake put away his "Landscapes" sketchbook, slipping it back inside the cellophane wrapper. He then opened up a new sketchbook. It would be called "Dragoneers."

CHAPTER 17

Samuel was a very observant man, and even though he didn't always comment on unusual occurrences, he was always aware of his surroundings and noticed things others may have missed. The attempted break-in had left many unanswered questions in his mind. Regardless of the comical ending to the incident, whoever was behind it was obviously trying to send Sam a message.

It was one thing to try to break into a place and commit arson under the cloak of darkness, but this had occurred on a Friday afternoon along a busy thoroughfare, with a number of potential witnesses. The perpetrator had been driving an MTAC vehicle, and even though the vehicle was later reported as stolen, to Sam, it seemed a bit too bold an action for a random act of vandalism.

It appeared to Sam that MTAC was trying to make a statement, and that statement would have been, "If we can get to Big Sam, we can get to you!" had the attempt been successful. Fortunately for Sam, his store had been a cornerstone of the community for years, and his reputation of fairness and generosity was broadly known. People loved Sam, and several of them had reported the break-in to the police even before Jake had called it in.

Big Sam's store was a rallying point for those opposed to the total takeover of the agricultural industry by MTAC. He'd hosted a number of rallies there, so it was only a matter of time before his store showed up on their to-do list.

MTAC was the embodiment of agricultural bullying, dragging down farm values and saturating the market with cheap produce by essentially kneecapping anyone trying to compete with them in the agricultural and dairy farming industries.

They'd obviously greased the palms of some public officials who were willing to turn a blind eye to that which was obvious to everyone else. All the while, MTAC maintained that they, like everyone else, were simply working the land. After all, in the eyes of the government, corporations were people too.

Sam was in a unique position, not actually being a farmer but still closely tied to them. Their success was also his success, and he did everything possible to make sure they had all the help they needed to be successful. This symbiotic relationship had proven fruitful over the years, benefitting the farmers and Sam's business equally.

Evidently, MTAC was now turning to outright extortion and vandalism to advance their agenda, operating with impunity in broad daylight, totally unconcerned with the consequences.

In Iraq, Samuel had grown accustomed to sneak attacks and attempts to sabotage the efforts of people like him who basically just wanted to make it back home to their loved ones. He understood that to beat them, you had to think as they did and even try to sabotage yourself to prevent anyone else from successfully doing so.

This was something in which Samuel, Jet, Baker, Ty, and Mac were all well-rehearsed. When you spent over a year in a foreign country protecting every inch of ground gained from an opponent who may be embedded with local allied forces during the day and attacking those same allies under the cloak of darkness each night, you learned to think outside the box.

The intruder who'd hit Sam's store used the only vulnerable entry point of the entire building. Over the past couple of years, Sam had been upgrading his security measures, and the reinforced steel replacement for the utility door damaged during the break-in had already been completed. It simply hadn't been installed yet, something the intruder had obviously either scoped out for himself or had been advised of by someone who had. In either case, this wasn't the work of an amateur. Bungled or not, this was a carefully planned attack foiled only by a five-pound dog who didn't back down.

In fact, Turbo had emboldened many of the farmers targeted by MTAC, causing them to reconsider their pending property sales. The video of Turbo posted on Sam's profile page was captioned "Resistance is *never* futile," and in the few days since posting it, Turbo's video had received over a million views and had been shared thousands of times, all to the obvious dismay of the MTAC board of directors.

The man who'd shown up at Sam's house asking questions about Turbo while claiming to work for a nonexistent publication was the only person photographed that day. Sam's surveillance cameras had captured numerous photos of him, giving him a series of clean images that he used for an internet reverse-image search.

Apparently, Svend Erickson was an alias for a private investigator named Svend Masterson. He seemed more like a mercenary than an investigator, suspected of having participated in a number of shady undertakings ranging from extortion to bribery. Although the common thread of his actions was a bit difficult to discern, it was obvious he was not a person to be trusted or taken lightly.

Sam had recognized the dangerous nature of the man hiding behind those ice-blue eyes and Scandinavian features. He'd been captured in images from Iceland and Norway as well as all over North and South America. There were also a few near matches in Beijing, China, and in Sydney, Australia, yet none of the image descriptions indicated exactly who or what he was associated with or what he was investigating.

While Samuel wasn't sure how or even *if* he was connected to MTAC, he was certain the man was dangerous and that he would be back, and the next time, he might not be so easy to get rid of. Regardless of his intentions, Sam would be ready.

Jake was well aware of his dad's concerns. His increased preoccupation with checking in on Jake and Sarah was obvious, even though there were no overt threats directed at either of them. Still, Jake trusted his father's intuition and took his concerns seriously.

T'Aer Bolun Dakkar had been exceptionally watchful since the day of the dragoneer's appearance. He carefully planned out their biweekly fishing trips, varying their departure days and times as well as their flight destinations and routes so as not to become predictable. Dragoneers never worked alone, realizing that capturing a dragon, even with a skilled team of experts, was extremely difficult. So far, T'Aer Bolun Dakkar had been able to identify four others in the local area, and since he was the only dragon within a thousand miles of Wilson

County, he knew they suspected his presence, even if they couldn't confirm it.

Working with T'Aer Bolun Dakkar, Jake had sketched out detailed drawings of each of the five dragoneers. Although he was unsure how he'd make use of the images at the time, he was certain it was important to have them.

That night's fishing excursion would be to the North Atlantic. Because of their varying time schedules, the trip would be a quick one, allowing them to depart at 2:00 a.m. and return before sunrise, no later than 5:00 a.m. T'Aer Bolun Dakkar had purposely chosen an overcast, moonless Saturday night to avoid detection upon their departure. The skies over the North Atlantic would be clear, giving them time to locate the herring swarms, feed, and return under the cover of the low-hanging clouds with plenty of time to spare.

He and Jake would need to make a trip down to the fishing cove before the clouds rolled in during the day. To maximize their stealth capability, T'Aer Bolun Dakkar would employ a method Jake had not yet experienced, and for that, he'd need to absorb plenty of sunlight.

CHAPTER 18

ON THE WAY down to the lake, Jake was admittedly worried about T'Aer Bolun Dakkar's plan. They'd be leaving two hours later than usual and still needed to be back before Jake's parents awakened. Since Samuel rose at five thirty every morning, they'd be cutting it close if anything unusual occurred along their route.

While T'Aer Bolun Dakkar assured Jake the he had a contingency plan, Jake was still very uneasy about the entire thing and was anxious to see how his dragon intended to cover their tracks if it became necessary. It wasn't that he doubted T'Aer Bolun Dakkar; he just needed reassurance to counter his own self-doubt and couldn't imagine what the dragon's plan would entail.

At the cove, Jake automatically headed toward his favorite fishing spot.

However, T'Aer Bolun Dakkar said, "No. We need to go to the opposite side of the cove today. We'll need full exposure to the sunlight for nearly two hours."

Heeding the dragon's words, Jake headed toward the opposite side of the cove. Once there, they continued up the bank through the woods, arriving at a wide-open pasture at the top of the hill. The pasture was about an acre large, covered in wild grasses and flowers. As T'Aer Bolun Dakkar had indicated, the area would be fully exposed to the sun for over two hours. What he hadn't indicated was that they would be fully exposed as well.

Jake was a bit taken aback as T'Aer Bolun Dakkar unfolded, revealing himself completely in the sun-soaked pasture. It was the first time he'd ever seen the dragon in full sunlight. As he lay down in the grass, even standing just a few feet from him, the dragon nearly disappeared completely in the grass. His camouflaged scales were so adaptive to the surroundings, it was nearly impossible to see him, even when you knew where he was.

"You must also charge your armor, Jake," said T'Aer Bolun Dakkar. "You'll need to remove your clothing so your scales are completely exposed to the sunlight."

Doing as instructed, Jake removed his clothing, exposing his armor to the sun. To his surprise and amazement, he all but vanished. The scales of his armor reacted so quickly to sunlight, he could barely discern the shape of his own hand as he held it out in front of his face. Even though Jake knew exactly where T'Aer Bolun Dakkar was lying in the grass, the dragon was also invisible to Jake.

"It takes some time to get adjusted, but your eyes will adapt soon, and you'll be able to distinguish between your body and the background surfaces and objects," explained T'Aer Bolun Dakkar.

"Is this why we need to charge the armor with sunlight?" asked Jake.

"No," replied the dragon. "Our armor can do this in any direct light if we so choose. It is less noticeable at night because of the darkened surroundings and near-complete dilation of the pupils. However, in direct sunlight, the pupils constrict, making it more difficult for you to see even your own physical contours."

"Wow!" exclaimed Jake. "This is unbelievable! How does it work?"

"As you noticed when we met initially, the scales on each side of my body are identical. For each scale on my right side, there is an exact mirror image of it on the left, each of which can both absorb and refract light. The two matching scales are interconnected through a dense nervous system that allows them to absorb light from one side of my body and project that light in the exact same intensity to the paired scale on the opposite side of my body. Each scale can act as both a projector and a screen simultaneously, making me essentially transparent," explained T'Aer Bolun Dakkar.

"But I didn't even try to be invisible," said Jake.

Suddenly, he reappeared, his body armor returning to deep shades of black and gray.

"What happened?" asked Jake.

"When necessary, I can activate your armor for you in case you're injured or incapacitated—but only if you are not actively controlling the change yourself. I've simply relinquished control to you," explained T'Aer Bolun Dakkar.

Sure enough, with only a thought, Jake vanished again completely.

"This is incredible," said Jake. "Can I do the same for you in the event of an emergency?"

"If I am incapacitated and cannot control the change myself, our bond allows you to initiate it for me and maintain it until I am able to retake control of my thoughts. However, your armor must be fully deployed for you to control mine, and even then, you can only make me vanish if you also vanish," explained the dragon.

After nearly two hours in the sun, T'Aer Bolun Dakkar rose from the ground, uncloaking and returning to the form of Turbo. Jake also dressed, and the two of them began the short journey back to the house.

"So if the sun bath had nothing to do with the cloaking ability, then what was it for?" asked Jake.

"For that, we'll need to wait until it's dark outside," answered T'Aer Bolun Dakkar.

Later that evening after dinner and movie night, Jake and Turbo wished Samuel and Sarah good night and headed upstairs to bed. By 11:00 p.m., Jake's parents had also gone to bed, and by midnight, they were sleeping deeply and peacefully.

At 1:45 a.m., both Jake and Turbo awakened simultaneously. Although they were both wide awake, T'Aer Bolun Dakkar told Jake to remain in his sleeping position and to deploy his armor. After doing so, the dragon instructed him to envision himself standing next to the bed, watching over his own body still lying there, asleep.

"Open your eyes," said T'Aer Bolun Dakkar.

As Jake opened his eyes, he was indeed standing next to his bed. Looking down, he could see himself still lying there in bed, asleep. At the foot of the bed, Turbo was curled up next to his feet, also sound asleep.

"Let's go," said Turbo, still in the shape of a dog but wearing scaly body armor.

Downstairs in the backyard, T'Aer Bolun Dakkar unfolded completely, lowering his left wing to the ground for Jake to mount.

Seconds later, they were a part of the overcast, moonless black sky, rapidly taking on altitude far above the flight paths of commercial airlines.

For Jake, it was still astounding how fast T'Aer Bolun Dakkar could fly. Above the cloud cover, the sky was crystal clear and littered with stars. Looking down at the dragon beneath him, Jake realized what he'd been told while sunbathing at the cove the day before was indeed true. While T'Aer Bolun Dakkar's contours were visible to Jake, he was indeed nearly invisible.

With merely a thought, Jake cloaked instantly as they left the North American continent far behind them. Minutes later, they were diving, plunging deep into the icy black waters of the North Atlantic. Quickly corralling and devouring the targeted bait ball, they were airborne again within minutes.

With the earth's rotation bringing Tennessee toward them, the return flight was even faster, and with an hour to spare, they were descending into the clouds covering the Mid-South when T'Aer Bolun Dakkar unexpectedly swerved sharply to the left.

Seconds later, what appeared to be a surface-to-air missile sailed up through the clouds directly into the path they'd just abandoned. Although it wasn't actually even a "near" miss, the mere fact that they'd detected T'Aer Bolun Dakkar's position inside the clouds during their descent meant their tracking techniques were getting better.

T'Aer Bolun Dakkar made the remainder of his approach absolutely unpredictable. Flying at treetop level, hugging the canopy of the thick forest, he circled the area erratically before approaching from the north, landing quietly in the forest a few hundred feet from Jake's backyard.

Downstairs, the light in the guest bathroom came on. Sam had awakened early and was using the downstairs bathroom, something he did to keep from waking Sarah, who was still sleeping upstairs. Remaining cloaked, Jake and Turbo silently crept up the stairs, disappearing into Jake's bedroom without so much as a peep. Upon their entering the room, the holographic avatars of Jake and Turbo sat up groggily, looking toward the door for a moment before apparently falling back to sleep. As they uncloaked, the holograms disappeared, with Jake and Turbo reclaiming their spots on the bed.

"That was a little too close for comfort," said Jake.

"No. I have avoided much faster projectiles in my time," replied T'Aer Bolun Dakkar.

"I was talking about Dad downstairs," responded Jake.

"The holograms would have lasted another hour easily," said T'Aer Bolun Dakkar. "We'll consider different options later today, but for now, we should rest. We have much to investigate."

"Agreed," said Jake.

Their departure had gone undetected, and they were both unshaken by the attempted air strike. Surprisingly, they both fell asleep quickly and without a care.

CHAPTER 19

LATER THAT MORNING, Jake and Turbo headed downstairs, where Sarah had prepared a hearty Southern-style breakfast of bacon, scrambled eggs with cheese, hominy grits, and homemade biscuits with butter and honey. This was Samuel's favorite breakfast, and Sarah enjoyed making it for him every Sunday morning.

After washing his hands, Jake set the table for breakfast, and Turbo curled up in his day bed on the floor near Jake. Sam, who had been in the living room, reading the Sunday paper and sipping his first cup of coffee, joined them, blessing the meal.

After serving everyone and taking her seat at the table, Sarah said, "We should go over to the Harvest Festival at the fairground this afternoon. I'd like to stock up on some preserves, molasses, and honey and just enjoy this beautiful autumn weather."

"You know, that's a great idea," said Sam. "I was just reading about it in the paper, and I love the way it smells there, with all the different kinds of food and candles and hobby crafts and such."

"Mrs. Nelson is going to be there with some of the things from our art class," said Jake. "She's auctioning them off for charity, so I donated some of my sketches. Maybe we can stop by her stand to say hello."

Mrs. Nelson was Jake's favorite teacher. Aside from Samuel and Sarah, she seemed to understand Jake better than anyone and encouraged him to express himself through his artwork.

"That's great, Jake!" said Sarah. "We'll most definitely peek in on her."

After breakfast, Jake helped his mom clear the table before heading outside. "I'm taking Turbo for a walk," he said.

"Be back by one o'clock so we can get to the Harvest Festival before everything's gone," said Sarah as the two of them headed out the door.

"Yes, ma'am," said Jake as he and Turbo left, closing the door behind them.

Walking down the lane, Jake took in the brisk autumn air while admiring the rich red and gold colors of the trees decorating the hillsides in the distance. The overcast sky provided a natural gray canvas that allowed the brightly colored leaves to really stand out against it.

Replaying the event in his mind, Jake asked T'Aer Bolun Dakkar, "How was it that the dragoneers were able to track us last night?"

"Just because we were invisible doesn't mean we weren't there," replied the dragon.

"But wouldn't they need to know our position to shoot at us?" asked Jake.

"Just because you can't see something doesn't mean it can't be detected. I believe the launch was triggered automatically because there was no one near the launch site," said T'Aer Bolun Dakkar.

"How do you know that?" asked Jake, still confused.

"I watched the launch and waited to see if anyone was observing from that location before I veered off the projectile's path. There was not, which indicates the launch was either triggered automatically or remotely," explained T'Aer Bolun Dakkar. "I believe they may have deployed several of these missiles at different approach vectors in hopes of getting lucky."

"That would make sense," said Jake. "There could be several of them in preset locations, armed and waiting, merely on the chance we'd cross the path of one of them."

"Precisely," said T'Aer Bolun Dakkar. "Even a miss offers them clues about where to concentrate their search. Obviously, the projectile wasn't armed with an explosive because they'd never risk one of those things coming down and exploding in a populated area."

"That make sense," said Jake, adding, "Even so, they'd probably want to recover it wherever it came down just to avoid arousing suspicion with the authorities."

"That's how we'll find them," said T'Aer Bolun Dakkar. "We'll follow the next missile to see where it comes down and wait to see who recovers it."

"The 'next' missile?" asked Jake. "So you're telling me we'll have to let them shoot at us again?"

"Precisely," replied T'Aer Bolun Dakkar.

"Cool!" said Jake excitedly as he and Turbo made their way back to the house.

That afternoon, the four of them climbed into Samuel's truck and drove over to the Harvest Festival. As always, the fairground was packed with people wearing coats, sweaters, and scarves while casually strolling through the maze of tents and vendor stands in the cool autumn weather.

In addition to the roller coaster, Ferris wheel, and other amusement rides, there were truck farmers selling fruits and vegetables, home-canned jellies and preserves, molasses and honey, baked goods, smoked hams, and other products grown and harvested right there in the local farming community. Each stand had its own uniquely mesmerizing scent, and combined, the aroma they created was heavenly.

T'Aer Bolun Dakkar had never experienced such an amazing collection of people. Everyone seemed to know one another in one way or another, and the feeling of belonging among them was profound. Even the vendors who were there selling their goods would leave their stands in the hands of their colleagues to wander the fairgrounds, visiting the stands of their friends and neighbors.

The counterclockwise flow of the pedestrian traffic allowed everyone the opportunity to see all the vendors while wandering the long looped circumference of the fairground. The amusement rides were located at the back of the loop, opposite the main entrance gate.

Looking up at the Ferris wheel, Jake smiled, remembering how only last year, he would have been far too afraid to ride something that high up into the air. The double-looped roller coaster would have been completely out of the question.

As Jake was staring up at the rides, Samuel asked, "Do you want to give it a shot this year?"

"Yes!" exclaimed Jake, surprising both Samuel and Sarah with his enthusiasm.

Leaving Turbo with his parents, Jake boarded the Ferris wheel for the first time ever. Purely by chance, he was seated in an empty seat next to Danni, a young girl from his math class.

"Hi, Jake," said Danni as the safety bar was lowered and locked in across their laps. "I'm Danni, from—"

"From math class," interjected Jake. "You sit two rows up from me, two seats to the right."

"Yes, that's right," said Danni, wrinkling her forehead after thinking about it for a second. "I'm surprised you noticed," she added, smiling.

"It's your hair," said Jake. "It reminds me of the hay in Grandpa's barn. I used to sneak out there and sleep in the loft when I was a kid." Jake was thinking that it was a silly thing to say.

In his mind, Jake heard T'Aer Bolun Dakkar telling him, "Actually, I think it may have been perfect."

"Really?" said Danni, smiling. "In a strange way, that may be one of the sweetest things anyone's ever said to me."

Jake was smiling and blushing as he replied, "There's no way that can be true. People say nice things about you all the time."

"*About* me. Not *to* me," Danni replied. "At times, I feel like a basket of apples or a sack of feed being compared by people at a farmer's market."

"Not much of a comparison there," said Jake, looking out across the countryside as their seat climbed higher and higher into the air. "It seems to me you're pretty much one of a kind."

"Thank you, Jake," said Danni, looking down and tucking her hair behind her ear. "You're pretty unique yourself."

"So I've heard," said Jake smiling.

"You know what I mean," said Danni, grinning and punching his arm playfully.

"Now you're trying to beat me up too," said Jake, smiling from ear to ear.

"You're impossible!" said Danni, laughing.

"I'd have thought *this* was impossible ten minutes ago," replied Jake. "Sitting next to the prettiest girl in my class, watching her smile at me, was right up there with getting struck by lightning while indoors."

"I'm glad you were wrong," said Danni. "Not about the lightning part, but the rest was very sweet."

Laughing together, they all but forgot they were riding the Ferris wheel. As the ride neared its end, Danni looped her arm into Jake's, resting her head on his shoulder. When the operator unlocked the seating bar and released it, she quickly kissed him on the cheek before they exited the ride.

"See you at school tomorrow," she said, skipping off toward her parents after looking back to smile at Jake one more time.

"How'd you like it?" asked Sam as Jake approached them.

"It was great," replied Jake. "Nothing to be afraid of at all."

Leaving the amusement ride area, Jake, his parents, and Turbo continued on along the pedestrian loop. A few yards farther down the walkway, they approached Mrs. Nelson's tent. Spotting them first, she waved frantically at Jake and his parents, calling them over.

"Hi, Jake!" she said excitedly.

"Hi, Mrs. Nelson. This is my mom and dad," said Jake as they each shook her hand in turn, formally introducing themselves.

"It's so wonderful to finally meet you both," said Mrs. Nelson. "Your son is an amazing artist, Mr. and Mrs. Payne."

"Thank you," said Sarah, looking around at the artwork on display, donated by her students.

"If you're looking for Jake's drawings, you won't find them in the display area anymore," said Mrs. Nelson. "They all went during the first auction."

"*What?*" said Sarah and Sam simultaneously.

"Yes!" said Mrs. Nelson. "The bidding started at the five-dollar minimum, and not one of them sold for less than a hundred dollars. Two of them actually sold for double that amount."

"Are you serious?" asked Jake, the amazement clearly showing on his face. "All ten of them?"

"Every last one of them," said Mrs. Nelson, "and they went to nine different buyers."

"That is amazing!" said Sarah with a broad smile on her face.

"Julia Hawthorne was here earlier, and she personally bought the two larger ones to mount in the lobby of the Hawthorne Arms," added

Mrs. Nelson. "In fact, she'll be coming to the school tomorrow to pay for and collect the paintings along with some other artwork she purchased today."

"That's wonderful!" said Sarah, beaming with pride. "I wish I could have seen them."

"I still have the ones for the Hawthorne," Jake's teacher said. "They're in the back. I'll get them for you to look at."

Disappearing into the back of the tent, she returned moments later with the two large drawings mounted inside simple glass frames. As Sam and Sarah stood there, staring at them in sheer amazement, Jake felt a sense of pride and accomplishment he'd never known before.

The drawings were of the tree-lined pasture across from Jake's bedroom window. It captured the storm front moving in from the east just before the rain began to fall. The panoramic view of the pasture was so wide, Jake had divided the image into two separate and distinct drawings, which, when viewed together, captured the intensity of the impending storm as if it were a living thing.

In the first image, the dark angry clouds looming over a peaceful field of purple and yellow flowers rolled in from the east behind a majestic stand of tall pine trees. In the second image, the sun was setting in the west, still reaching out with beautiful rays of light in resolute defiance of the approaching storm. The two images seemed to be moving toward each other, capturing a moment that was mesmerizingly powerful.

"Oh my god, Jake," said Sarah. "These are the most incredible images I've ever seen."

"They are magical," said Mrs. Nelson. "Every person who passed by them was compelled to stop, even after they were marked as sold. People were literally transfixed, staring at them for minutes on end, as if unable to move from the spot."

"I'll bet," said Sam, still staring at the two drawings himself. "It's as if you're standing in that field, flanked on each side by the powers of darkness and light, not knowing which of the two will be victorious."

"The light will always win," said Jake. "Storm clouds will come from time to time, but no matter how hard they try to block out the sun, within a few hours, it'll be back, rising up from behind them as they scurry off into nothingness."

"Well said," replied Samuel, placing his large hand on Jake's shoulder. "Now speaking of scurrying, it's time we get going. You have school tomorrow, and we need to figure out what to do with all the stuff your mom bought when we get home."

"Good night, Mrs. Nelson," said Jake. "I'll see you in class tomorrow."

"Good night, Jake, and it was nice to meet you, Mr. and Mrs. Payne," replied Mrs. Nelson, waving to them as they headed back toward the main gate, where people were beginning to file out of the fairgrounds.

In Samuel's truck, Jake's parents spoke softly with each other on the way home about the things Sarah had purchased and the bargain prices she'd paid for them. In the back seat, Turbo was asleep, and Jake was staring blankly out the window, remembering the excitement of his very first kiss.

CHAPTER 20

JAKE WAS UNUSUALLY quiet on the way to school on Monday morning, conversing neither aloud with Sam nor telepathically with T'Aer Bolun Dakkar. They were already pulling up to the front of the school when he finally broke the silence.

"Dad, if a girl kisses you on the cheek, does that make her your girlfriend?" asked Jake.

"The only thing that makes a girl your girlfriend is if you respectfully ask her to be and she agrees. However, if she's already kissed you on the cheek and you like her, then you've already got a running start," answered Sam.

Nodding silently, Jake opened the door of the truck to get out.

Before he closed it behind him, Sam said, "Hey."

Sticking his head back inside the truck, Jake said, "Yes, sir?"

"Is she pretty?" asked Sam.

"Do you remember my two drawings from yesterday?" asked Jake.

Nodding, Sam answered, "Of course. That's something I'll likely never forget."

"She's the sunny one," replied Jake, smiling as he closed the door behind him and headed up the front steps into the school building.

"Oh yeah. She's pretty," said Sam, looking down at Turbo on the seat next to him as they headed out of the parking lot on the way to the store.

Jet and Baker were already there, opening up the store, when Sam and Turbo arrived. Having spent the past few evenings working on a security upgrade for the store, Jet was excited to show Sam and Baker how it worked.

Having been an air force fire protection specialist, Jet had worked with architects and design engineers in developing specialized fire suppression systems for aircraft hangars and weapons storage facilities. These facilities, by their very nature, were extremely vulnerable to damage by fire and were always at the top of enemy targeting lists.

In the case of many of the highly flammable products in Big Sam's store, standard overhead sprinkler systems would be ineffective for some of them and highly damaging to others. Therefore, the best means of protecting these types of products and facilities was by quenching any fires immediately and effectively preventing them from rekindling.

To that end, Jet had designed and installed a customized carbon dioxide flush system that would instantly rob any fire of the one thing it required to burn—oxygen. Furthermore, it could be armed and activated either remotely or when sensors inside the store detected a fire. Once activated, it would extinguish the fire within seconds.

As Jet prepared for the demonstration, everyone else left the store and waited outside in the parking lot. Sam monitored him via the remote surveillance system using his tablet, while Jet lit twenty "trick" birthday candles and placed them at different locations throughout the store. Unlike normal candles, these candles would reignite themselves after having been blown out. Having disarmed the alarm and sprinkler systems for the test, Sam was anxious to see how well the system would work.

After a few minutes, Jet joined everyone outside in the parking lot, giving Sam the thumbs up to activate the remote sensor monitor. Since the candles were already burning, the sensors lit up immediately, indicating the presence of fire in multiple locations throughout the interior of the building.

As they watched on Sam's tablet, he hit the flashing red icon on his touch screen. The exterior air vents sealed immediately, and the store was instantly flushed with carbon dioxide from multiple ports inside the building. Within seven seconds, every candle had been extinguished.

Outside, everyone held their breath, waiting to see if the candles would reignite. They did not, and the three men in the parking lot with Turbo broke into applause, high-fiving one another for the successful systems test.

Before going back into the store, Jet cautioned everyone, "Always reopen the air vents before going back inside the building once the fire has been completely extinguished. Otherwise, you could end up suffocating after having survived the fire."

"Got it," said Sam. "Great job, Jet!"

After waiting a few minutes to reenter the store, the three men and Turbo walked through the entire building, confirming, as Jet had ensured them, nothing had been damaged.

At Jake's school, his first period, English class, was just ending, and his heart was racing as he headed to his second period, math class. Cautiously opening the door at the rear of the classroom just enough to peek in, he noticed Danni wasn't at her desk yet.

"Looking for me?" came the familiar voice from behind him as he turned to find Danni standing there, smiling.

"To be honest, yes, I *was* looking for you," said Jake, feeling strangely awkward.

"Well, here I am," said Danni. "What's next?"

"Would you be my girlfriend?" asked Jake, blushing as his heartbeat thundered inside his chest.

"Well, how about I think it over while you hold my hand and walk me to math class?" said Danni.

"But we're already here," said Jake, dazed and somewhat confused.

"Through the front door, Jake," said Danni. "I'm not afraid to show off my boyfriend."

Smiling, Jake held out his hand, which Danni took without hesitation. When they walked into the classroom together, a hush fell over the entire room as Jake walked Danni to her seat before taking his, two rows back and two seats to the left of her.

"Beautifully done," said T'Aer Bolun Dakkar, who'd been observing the entire time without interfering. "She really is the sunshine."

"Thanks," said Jake, smiling to himself.

As the bell rang, Danni glanced back at Jake one final time before the teacher walked into the room. Approaching her desk slowly, the teacher skeptically looked around the classroom in paranoid disbelief. It was so quiet, you could have heard a pin drop.

CHAPTER 21

HAVING ALREADY TRIGGERED the auto-launch of one missile, T'Aer Bolun Dakkar wanted to avoid the possibility of triangulation, which could lead the dragoneers back to Jake's doorstep. It was one thing for them to investigate the unsubstantiated claims of an attempted arsonist; however, arousing further suspicions that led them to the same point of interest would be too great a coincidence for them to simply dismiss. Therefore, T'Aer Bolun Dakkar would need to be exceedingly cautious to avoid having to deal with them directly.

Fortunately, dragons were as well equipped to avoid unwanted conflicts with adversaries as they were to engage them with extreme malice. Given an option, dragons would always choose evasion over confrontation.

Their next fishing trip would be radically different from anything Jake had ever experienced with T'Aer Bolun Dakkar. With it being Thanksgiving week, Jake only had school on Monday and Tuesday, so they would plan their trip for Tuesday night.

Despite having Danni on his mind for the majority of the time, Jake was diligent in his research, trying to determine how the dragoneers had managed to track them. They had most definitely not been seen because to the naked eye, they were invisible without a doubt. The beating of T'Aer Bolun Dakkar's wings could not have been a factor either as during their descent, they were tightly pressed against his sides, deployed only to change direction, seconds before the missile would have impacted them.

It took him a while, but he surmised it must have been something very specific that had led them to T'Aer Bolun Dakkar.

"How did you know when Tao Min Xiong was near?" Jake asked T'Aer Bolun Dakkar.

"The armor of related or bonded dragons alerts and attracts us to one another, while the armor of unrelated dragons creates a magnetic field that repels and allows us to maintain an appropriate territorial distance from one another," answered T'Aer Bolun Dakkar.

"So basically, Tao Min Xiong's armor repels yours—" started Jake.

"No," interrupted T'Aer Bolun Dakkar. "I avoided Tao Min Xiong solely out of respect for his status and tenure. His armor actually attracted ours."

Curiously, Jake asked, "Are you saying..."

"Yes," responded T'Aer Bolun Dakkar. "We are related." Turning to look at Jake, he added, "Tao Min Xiong is my father."

"But if Tao Min Xiong is your father, then you too are a dragon king," replied Jake, astonished.

"I am a dragon king ascendant," replied T'Aer Bolun Dakkar. "Tao Min Xiong was my mother's mate."

In the silence that followed, Jake's mind analyzed and connected the genealogical data based on what he'd learned of dragons from T'Aer Bolun Dakkar. There were only four dragon kings, each reigning for an era of a thousand years, beginning at or near their one-hundredth birthday.

"We were together the very first time you saw your father," said Jake. "Why didn't you tell me?"

T'Aer Bolun Dakkar looked at Jake, saying, "Neither you nor I was ready to approach the subject at that time. Even now, we are unprepared as the task at hand requires our immediate attention."

As always, Jake realized T'Aer Bolun Dakkar was correct, and now, more than ever, they needed to complete their mission to protect not only Jake's family but also the heir to one of only four dragon kingdoms.

As Jake refocused on his research, his theory was that the dragoneers must have been in possession of either the scales of a dragon or the person to which a dragon had been bonded. Either way, that knowledge would be highly useful in understanding how they may have been able to target T'Aer Bolun Dakkar.

That night, after Samuel and Sarah were asleep, Jake and T'Aer Bolun Dakkar left the house and headed down to the cove. Once there, they entered the lake. As they submerged, Jake clung to the dragon's neck, gliding along the bottom of the relatively shallow lake at amazing speed. Leaving the water only to maneuver past locks and dams, they entered the Cumberland River, navigating north to where it merged into the Ohio River. Guided by T'Aer Bolun Dakkar's unerring genetic sensory navigation, they were soon blistering down the Mississippi River, just below the surface.

Only minutes after they had followed the river past New Orleans, the presence of saline in the water marked their entry into the Gulf of Mexico. A hundred miles out into the gulf, Jake and T'Aer Bolun Dakkar exited the water, taking flight across the Florida peninsula before descending into the welcoming heart of the Atlantic Ocean, a hundred miles off the coast of Bermuda.

After T'Aer Bolun Dakkar had gorged himself on Atlantic herring, they remained submerged, heading north around Bay Saint Lawrence and Meat Cove and then west toward New Brunswick, where they exited the water, taking flight over Quebec City and Montreal. Remaining at high altitude, they allowed the earth's rotation to bring Tennessee toward them before rapidly descending into the area between Lexington, Kentucky, and Nashville, Tennessee.

As expected, T'Aer Bolun Dakkar saw the flash of the launcher as the missile was deployed, headed directly at them. This time, T'Aer Bolun Dakkar waited until the missile was nearly upon them before making his evasive maneuver. As the projectile jetted past them, they followed its path, watching this time as a parachute was deployed, allowing it to float gently to the ground.

After marking its location, T'Aer Bolun Dakkar headed north, back into Canadian airspace, before descending to sea level off the coast of Nova Scotia. Following the coastline back down to Charleston, South Carolina, at extremely low altitude, they approached Tennessee from the southeast, landing unnoticed in the woods behind Jake's house just before 5:00 a.m.

If their plan worked, the dragoneers would be searching for a dragon hiding somewhere between Nova Scotia and New Brunswick, while the police would be investigating the launch site and landing point of a surface-to-air missile fired from inside U.S. airspace. The burn phone

Jake had used to call it in was now resting somewhere deep in the icy waters off the coast of New Hampshire.

Sam and Sarah were still asleep as they quietly climbed the stairs and disappeared into Jake's bedroom, where an ascendant dragon king fell asleep at the feet of a brilliant young man.

CHAPTER 22

JAKE AWOKE SLEEPILY on the morning of Thanksgiving Eve, having traveled thousands of miles the night before with T'Aer Bolun Dakkar. While the journey itself was absolutely spectacular, even T'Aer Bolun Dakkar was fatigued afterward.

As Jake made his way down the stairs, Turbo continued his extended slumber, recovering from the physical exertion that had severely drained him. In the kitchen, he found a note from Sarah letting him know she'd gone grocery shopping and would be back in a couple of hours as well as a covered plate of biscuits and smoked ham in the oven for him. Pouring himself a glass of milk, he took the plate and sat in a stool at the counter between the kitchen and the living room. He noticed the television remote on the countertop and casually turned on the TV while he ate.

Halfway through the meal, he noticed a special report on the cable news channel his mom had left running in the background most of the day. His eyes widening in near disbelief, Jake nearly choked on his milk as he recognized Svend Erickson as one of the people being led away in handcuffs by FBI agents on the screen. Looking closer, he recognized all of them.

Nearly leaping from the stool, Jake rushed back up the stairs into his bedroom. As he retrieved his "Dragoneers" sketchbook from the bottom shelf of his nightstand, Turbo groggily lifted his head, observing Jake's obvious excitement.

"What has you so excited, young Jake?" asked T'Aer Bolun Dakkar through sleep-crusted eyes.

Grabbing the seldom-used remote, he turned on the television in his room, switching to the cable news station. On the screen, the network was replaying the recorded apprehension of the five individuals they'd arrested in an overnight sting operation.

"Look! They're the same people I drew in my sketchbook!" said Jake, flipping through the spitting images he'd created of the five people the authorities had arrested during the operation.

Based on an anonymous tip phoned in by a concerned citizen, they were able to pinpoint both the location of the launch site and the recovery zone of the projectile. Evidently, the first missile had not gone unnoticed by homeland security officers, who suspected the launch had been a terrorist training run, potentially aimed at bringing down a commercial aircraft. While the projectile itself was not equipped with an explosive warhead, it was fitted with a glass cylinder containing an oily yellow liquid, the composition of which had yet to be determined.

"Oleander oil," said T'Aer Bolun Dakkar. "Had it impacted us, the glass would have shattered, atomizing the oil into a very fine mist, which..."

"Would have killed you," finished Jake.

"Yes," replied T'Aer Bolun Dakkar. "It would have killed both of us."

"Well, it would appear your speed and maneuverability were something they hadn't counted on in selecting this method of attack," said Jake.

"And your suggestion to use the commercial flight path from Lexington to Nashville ensured the projectile would be noticed by other aircraft and ATC control towers," said T'Aer Bolun Dakkar. "Well done."

At the store, Sam and his crew were watching intently as the news story continued to develop throughout the day.

"I knew there was something odd about that guy when he showed up at my house, out of the blue, on a Sunday afternoon," said Sam. "I'm just glad they caught them before they could harm anyone."

"Amen to that!" said Baker. "But if we don't get this store flipped and ready for tomorrow's Thanksgiving dinner, Sarah is going to have all our heads on a silver platter," he added, laughing.

For the past ten years, Sarah and Big Sam had hosted their holiday kickoff dinner at the store on Thanksgiving Day. In addition to a holiday spread hosted and supported by other local businesses and sponsors, the event marked the start of the annual toy drive, featuring a tree-lighting ceremony and the official reveal of "Sam-ta's Workshop." From Thanksgiving Day through Christmas Eve, Big Sam collected toys and donations for underprivileged children and needy families from across the county. For Sam-ta's Workshop, the equipment repair bays at the back of the building were emptied out, and the space was converted into a veritable winter wonderland.

The center of the huge warehouse was a wide-open space with a thirty-foot ceiling. Around the perimeter were two levels of balconies that allowed large vehicles such as large combine harvesters and heavy equipment vehicles to be rolled in and worked on from different levels. For Sam-ta's Workshop, a giant natural Christmas tree was raised in the center of the warehouse, and the individual work bays on each level were designated for the different types of items donated.

With the exception of Sam's employees and the team from the company who volunteered to decorate it, no one was allowed into the warehouse from Monday through Thursday the week of Thanksgiving until the big reveal.

Within days, the festively decorated though empty warehouse would be transformed into a magical paradise as people and companies from all over the state delivered food, toys, shoes, clothing, and gift cards, literally filling Sam-ta's Workshop to the ceiling with gifts and donations.

The front of the store was a totally different story. That part of the project was Sarah's and Sarah's alone. For the dinner, the merchandise shelves were all moved to the outer edges of the store and closed off with decorative pipe and drape, creating a large open space in the center of the retail area.

Over the past decade, schools from all over the county had gotten involved, donating artistically decorated four-foot-by-eight-foot drape segments to replace what had started off as a plain white background. The donated segments were entered into a contest, and the winning school's art class was awarded a pizza-party field trip at a local pizzeria when they returned to school after the Christmas and New Year's break.

In the center of the room, Sarah created a visual masterpiece using items she'd purchased at the Harvest Festival and from local retailers participating in the Thanksgiving Day event. During the first two years, she'd personally prepared all the food for the dinner; however, after the event exploded into a community "happening," food donations began pouring in from restaurants and grocery stores all over Wilson County.

While Sarah prepared everything inside the store, managing and organizing the food service personnel and catering professionals, Sam, Jet, Baker, Ty, and Mac worked on the outside, adding music, lights, and other eye-catching Christmas decorations on and around the entire building. By late Wednesday evening, Big Sam's was unrecognizable, having been totally transformed inside and out.

Jake was more excited than anyone about this year's kickoff event. Danni's parents had been donating products and services to Sam-ta's Workshop for the past several years, but this year, she was going to be there, and he was really looking forward to seeing her.

T'Aer Bolun Dakkar was exceptionally curious about the traditions of Thanksgiving Day, having never had either a reason or an opportunity to experience it firsthand. While Jake's excitement in regard to the event was certainly infectious, it was difficult to distinguish between his degree of zeal for the party and his obvious affection for Danni. Either way, it would provide another opportunity for T'Aer Bolun Dakkar to directly interact with people in a festive social setting.

That evening, Sam and Sarah brought home pizza for dinner, which everyone ate in the living room while watching Christmas specials on television. Afterward, they exchanged testimonies in turn, listing the things for which they were thankful.

Sam was grateful for his family and friends and their continued prosperity even in the face of difficult times. Sarah was thankful for her family's health and well-being and the unconditional love shared among them.

Jake was thankful for the trust and support he received from his parents on a daily basis and their diligence and hard work when it came to providing a safe and loving home for him. Even though he was admittedly challenging for them at times, he was grateful for their forgiving and understanding nature toward him.

Finally, looking down at the little dog sitting beside him on the floor, Jake said, smiling, "I'm thankful for you, Turbo, for helping me realize I can love and be loved by someone other than my parents and for giving me the confidence to become a better version of myself without judging me for my failures and my shortcomings."

On the floor, Turbo stared blankly at Jake sitting next to him. He had been totally unprepared for such a heartfelt public declaration of appreciation from Jake and was unable to resist the urge to thank him. Hopping onto Jake's lap, he placed his tiny little paws against Jake's chest and licked him on the chin.

In his mind, he said, "I love you, Jake."

"I know, T'Aer Bolun Dakkar," said Jake aloud for everyone to hear. "And I love you too."

T'Aer Bolun Dakkar already liked this "Thanksgiving" thing.

CHAPTER 23

THANKSGIVING DAY STARTED with a bang in the Payne household. Both Sam and Sarah were up before dawn, preparing for the big event. Even though Jake and Turbo were awake, they both took their time making their way downstairs, primarily to avoid being in Sarah's and Sam's way as they hustled through the house, collecting things and loading them into the back of Sam's truck.

Most of their activity was out of tradition more than anything else as the majority of the preparation had been completed the day before. There were, however, a few decorations and props Sarah had forgotten to take with her previously, and of course, Jake's dad was always very particular about one box whose contents no one other than he and Sarah had been able to view since as far back as Jake could remember. Even though Jake had figured it out four years prior, he always went along with the tradition, enjoying his part in keeping the "family secret."

By 10:00 a.m., everything and everyone had been loaded into Sam's truck, and they were all on the way to the store. Half an hour later, they were pulling into a parking lot that was already buzzing with activity. Jet and Baker had spent the night at the store directing the outdoor vendors to their lot spaces, some of whom had driven in from as far away as the eastern- and westernmost corners of the state.

Over the years, this little gathering had spilled over from only the inside of the store and had taken over the entire parking area and the lot surrounding the building. Although Sam never charged a fee to use the vendor spaces, they were reserved months in advance by vendors from all over the county and the state and were highly coveted. The majority of the proceeds went toward the charity, and all the vendors were more than happy to contribute their time and resources to this highly anticipated social event.

Inside, several long tables had been prepared for the official dinner, with beautiful place settings, tablecloths, and chair covers provided each year by the Hawthorne Arms Hotel. The porcelain dinnerware, crystal drinking glasses, cloth napkins, and ornate silver flatware were specifically selected to prevent the dinner from feeling like a handout for those families who'd managed to swallow their pride and ask for help.

This year, over fifty families had signed up for the dinner with plated service prepared for nearly three hundred people. The families arrived via shuttle service from several different participating churches just before 3:00 p.m., when the official dinner service began.

Sam, Sarah, Jake, and Turbo looked out across the tables with joy as their extended store family of military veterans was joined by families who'd been hit hard by the year's unforgiving agricultural market. Together, they were all able to enjoy a beautiful meal with their loved ones in this festive environment as skilled servers catered to their guests with obvious care and delight.

After the meal, the guests were invited to browse the vendor lot outside before it opened at 5:00 p.m., while the service crew cleared the dinner tables and prepared for the main event. With people slowly trickling in to wander through the lot ahead of the big reveal, by "go time," the place was buzzing with activity.

Shortly before the reveal, Sam was nowhere to be found, but walking in through the front door was another very familiar face: Danni, flanked by her parents, Julia and Richard Hawthorne. As Sarah greeted them warmly, thanking Julia for the beautiful place settings and decor, Jake was close behind her, smiling broadly.

"Hi, Jake!" exclaimed Danni excitedly, taking Jake's hand. "Let's go outside. I want to see everything."

In a flash, they were headed out the door, with Turbo close behind them. Outside, they were greeted by the smell of pine from the Christmas tree vendor and roasted chestnuts lingering in the brisk autumn air. Jake watched Danni with amusement as she darted from stand to stand in her long winter coat and scarf, dragging him happily behind her the whole way.

Five minutes before the reveal, Jet made the announcement over the public address system, inviting everyone inside for the main event. Indoors, while dozens of people gathered in the storefront, eyeing the dark curtains shielding the entrance to Sam-ta's Workshop, Turbo quietly slipped outside. Something wasn't right.

As the countdown clock ticked off the final few seconds, the crowd joined in, verbally calling out, "Ten . . . nine . . . eight . . . seven . . ."

Out in front of the building, a black unmarked SUV slowly approached the store, lowering its windows. It stopped directly in front of the now empty parking lot, and two men in pseudo-riot gear exited, shouldering rocket-propelled grenade launchers.

As the countdown echoed loudly in the air, Turbo charged off the front porch of the store into the parking lot.

"Three . . . two . . . one . . ."

Outside, the men fired their weapons, launching their deadly ordinance toward the windows of the crowded building as Turbo defiantly charged the vehicle.

Inside, the crowd erupted into a boisterous uproar, screaming loudly as the curtains fell, revealing the gloriously decorated tree in the center of an awe-inspiring Christmas paradise.

Outside, T'Aer Bolun Dakkar unfolded in front of the speeding projectiles. Spreading his massive wings and funneling both rockets in toward his impenetrable dragon hide, he completely engulfed them by wrapping his wings tightly around his torso. The sound of the exploding grenades didn't even penetrate the envelope of T'Aer Bolun Dakkar's embrace as they detonated harmlessly against his chest.

As T'Aer Bolun Dakkar unfolded his wings, the worthless shrapnel fell inertly to the ground at his feet. With a simple sweep of them from T'Aer Bolun Dakkar, the fragments were whisked into the gravel alongside the road as the masked men quickly jumped back into the SUV, speeding off to the sound of screeching tires. Inside the vehicle, the men were absolutely frantic.

"*What the hell just happened?*" screamed one of the attackers.

"*How the hell am I supposed to know?*" screamed the other. "The damn things just disappeared into nothing! It's like the night just swallowed them up!"

Suddenly, the driver realized he'd lost control of the vehicle's steering, and inside the SUV, the ceiling began crumpling downward, shattering the windows. As the passengers reached for the doors, they too crushed inward, making them impossible to open. The men were trapped inside an inescapable coffin of twisted steel.

Peering out the narrow slits of the compacted window openings, they realized they were being lifted high into the air. At times, the vehicle dangled steeply, swinging wildly through the air as the occupants were tossed about like jacks inside a cardboard box. Just as suddenly, they were falling, and the twisted vehicle came crashing down into the impound lot behind the sheriff's office.

Looking back over his wings, T'Aer Bolun Dakkar watched as deputies stormed out of the building into the half-empty lot, surrounding the vehicle. Within seconds, Turbo was trotting back inside through the front entrance of the store, where the party was in full swing.

Next to the Christmas tree, "Sam-ta" was sitting on a large gold-painted throne covered in red velvet that perfectly matched his custom-tailored outfit. Even beneath the frosty white beard and mustache, with the fur-lined hat pulled down to his eyebrows, Big Sam was easily recognizable to everyone in the room. No one else was even close to his size, and he was otherwise conspicuously missing from the rest of the crowd.

He smiled sincerely as he greeted children from the long line of kids that formed in front of him and listened intently as they whispered their Christmas wishes into his welcoming ear. Jet, Baker, Ty, Mac, and Sarah were acting as Sam-ta's helpers, appreciatively accepting donations from the vendors, which were already pouring into the various bays of the workshop, and the aura of compassion was thick in the air.

After a couple of hours, the line of kids had been whittled down to the last child standing. The shuttle buses were loaded and headed back to their respective churches with enough leftovers, boxed and canned goods, and frozen turkeys to carry each family through the coming weeks at a minimum. Volunteers were packing up their stands, and except for the Christmas tree vendor, most of them were right behind the shuttle buses as they quickly filed out of the lot.

Danni and her parents were among the last to leave, with Julia and Richard thanking Sam-ta and Sarah and asking her to pass their season's greetings on to Big Sam, wherever he might be hiding. Jake and Danni were outside on the porch together, smiling and giggling as they swung back and forth on the swing near the front door, with Turbo lying on the floor next to Jake's feet.

Baker had thoughtfully brought the Hawthornes' car and Sam's truck around to the front of the store earlier that evening after the lot had been cleared.

With a hug and a quick kiss on the cheek for Jake, Danni headed down the stairs with her parents, waving and saying, "Good night, Jake. Good night, Mr. and Mrs. Payne," and finally, "Good night, Turbo!"

Their car left the parking lot to the waves of everyone on the porch before Sam-ta and Sarah headed back inside.

On the porch, Jake asked T'Aer Bolun Dakkar, "Where did you go during the countdown? I lost you there for a moment."

"I was outside getting rid of some unwanted pests," replied T'Aer Bolun Dakkar. "Nothing worth taking you away from the celebration for, but I'll tell you all about it later tonight."

"Fair enough," said Jake, looking at Turbo, squinting suspiciously.

Just then, Sam and Sarah reemerged, with Sam holding his "secret" box under one arm. After he had placed it in the back, everyone piled into the truck, leaving the store in the capable hands of Jet, Baker, Ty, and Mac.

"Another one for the history books," said Sam, taking Sarah's hand on the center console.

"The countdown was awesome," said Sarah.

"So I heard," said Sam, smiling.

"Too bad you missed it," said Sarah.

"There's always next year," said Sam, squeezing Sarah's hand.

As they passed the sheriff's office, they barely even noticed the commotion or the flashing yellow lights of the wrecker winching the twisted remains of a black SUV onto its tilted flatbed.

CHAPTER 24

AFTER A FOUR-DAY weekend, Jake was happy about returning to school. He was excited about seeing Danni and also had something special to show Mrs. Nelson during art class.

Dropping Jake off at the school, Sam told Jake, "Have a great day, son, and we'll see you at the store after school."

"Thanks, Dad," said Jake before sprinting up the stairs to the front doors.

Sam and Turbo headed to the store, and in fewer than five minutes, they were turning into the parking lot of Big Sam's. Before they could exit their vehicle, Sam noticed the sheriff's cruiser pulling into the parking lot behind them. Getting out of his truck, he waited by the stairs as the sheriff exited his vehicle and approached the store.

"Good morning, Sheriff," said Sam, extending his arm and shaking the sheriff's hand. "What brings you out our way this morning?"

With one hand on his hip and the other adjusting his hat, the sheriff said, "I'm trying to make some sense out of something that makes no sense."

"Well, Sheriff, I've been trying to do that all my life in some form or other," said Samuel, smiling. "How can I help you?"

"On Thursday evening, my deputies cut three fellas out of a sardine can that used to be a brand-new Yukon from a car rental place in Nashville," said the sheriff. "The story they told the deputies was so bizarre, they called me into the office."

"What do you mean by bizarre?" asked Sam.

"Well, it seems that the Yukon was dropped off into the impound lot while the deputies on duty were enjoying some of the Thanksgiving dinner Sarah had Ty bring by for them."

"That's odd," said Sam. "Why were they still inside the car when the tow truck dropped it off?"

"Well, see, now that's the odd thing. There was no tow truck. The dang thing just fell out of the sky and dropped into the impound lot behind the building."

"How is that even possible?" asked Sam. "Were any of them injured?"

"Which brings us to oddity number two," said the sheriff. "Other than a few bumps, bruises, and ruffled feathers, they were all fine."

"Now you've lost me completely, Sheriff," said Sam. "The truck fell out of the sky and landed in your impound lot, but no one was hurt."

"See there, Sam? You're not lost at all. That's exactly what they claim happened. The crazy thing is the truck apparently *did* fall out of the sky, according to the surveillance cameras covering the impound lot," the sheriff explained. "We used a diamond saw to cut the roof off the truck and get them out."

"Okay, let's recap," said Sam, confused and scratching his head. "The truck was damaged so badly, the men inside couldn't get out of it, but somehow they managed to fly it and land it in your impound lot."

"I don't know if I'd quite call that a landing, but yeah, that's about the gist of it," said the sheriff. "Which brings us to oddity number three. Inside the Yukon, the deputies found two rocket-propelled grenade launchers that had been fired and three fully automatic assault rifles with about a thousand rounds of ammo in dozens of preloaded magazines."

"*Are you kidding me?*" asked Sam. "I haven't seen that kind of assault preparation since I left Iraq."

"And what kind of assault preparation would that be?" asked the sheriff.

"Well, first, you create pandemonium with the RPGs and then mow down all those terrified people when they attempt to flee the building," said Sam, his blank stare drifting off into the distance. "It's a very nasty tactic but very effective in terrorizing people. Who the heck would do such a thing on Thanksgiving Day?"

"Which brings us to oddity number four," said the sheriff. "The men in that vehicle were so traumatized, they were spilling their guts as we were cutting them out of the truck. It was crazy talk. They were jabbering about how the darkness opened up and swallowed the rockets. After that, they were too scared to stick around and tried to escape the scene pronto," he added. "They said they were hired by MTAC."

"What?" said Sam, wide-eyed. "Who was their target?"

"You," said the sheriff, pushing his cowboy hat back from his forehead and looking directly into Sam's eyes. "They said they attacked at 6:00 p.m. when your place was full of people."

"That cannot be!" exclaimed Sam. "I've been caught up in an explosion before. The blast from an RPG is so loud, it leaves your ears ringing for days. If anyone had fired one of those into the store or anywhere around it, you'd have felt the air compression for a block in every direction and heard the explosion even from miles away."

"You see, that's exactly what I thought, so I came down to your store around 2:00 a.m. with some crime scene investigators from the county. They were not very happy about being called out, but they actually found shards of shrapnel mixed in with the gravel alongside the road in front of your store. They said it was a positive match for the launchers and grenades found inside the vehicle."

Walking out to the edge of the road with the sheriff, Sam said, "You're telling me they actually fired those things at the store, but they exploded out here, next to the road?"

"Well, this is where they recovered the shrapnel," said the sheriff. "All of it, every single piece."

"That is very, very odd," said Samuel. "But I've seen it happen before. Once the Iraqi Army was defeated, there were still independent terrorists who attempted to cause mayhem whenever and wherever they could. The problem is without a military force to maintain their munitions, especially after the extended bombing campaigns, much of the ordinance was either damaged or defective, and when you purchase this stuff on the black market, you're taking a fifty-fifty chance on the odds it'll even work."

"Well, that's somewhere along the same lines the ballistics folks over at the county told me," said the sheriff. "The problem is these things *did* explode. The shrapnel they recovered was from the exploded grenades. Had the rockets failed and the grenades landed here, the explosion would have sent the shrapnel into everything around it, including the Yukon, which, by the way, had no signs of being damaged by shrapnel from the exploding grenades."

The two men stood out next to the road, kicking through the gravel as if looking for more shrapnel. Turbo observed them from the porch, listening to every word of the conversation dispassionately while memorizing every single detail.

"We just finished upgrading our security and surveillance systems, and I'm sure that if they fired grenades or anything else at the store, my surveillance cameras would have caught it," said Samuel. "Come on inside, Sheriff. I'll get you some of our coffee—if you can handle Baker's military grade brew. We can pull up the video feed from my security cloud and review it right here."

A few minutes later, Samuel and the sheriff were locked in the administration office, reviewing the video, with Turbo sitting underneath the desk. Sure enough, the recording showed eight different camera feeds, with the black Yukon slowly pulling up on the otherwise empty road out in front of the store.

As everyone inside was counting down for the big reveal, the occupants stepped out of the Yukon and fired. Sure enough, the rockets simply disappeared into thin air–no explosion, no flying shrapnel, nothing. The assailants literally stumbled over one another trying to get back into the truck before it sped off down the road and out of the range of Sam's cameras.

Just as Sam was about to pause the recording, he noticed something that had stopped him cold, zooming in closer while the shooters were scrambling for their vehicle. The grenade fragments and shrapnel could be seen falling to the ground out of thin air and then apparently being swept into the gravel alongside the road. It really *did* look like the darkness had swallowed up the rockets and then spat out the shrapnel without it ever exploding.

"This is way above my pay grade," said Sam. "I'd be happy to email all this footage over to your office so you and the county CSI can analyze it, but this is definitely not something I could write off as faulty black-market ammunition. I have never seen anything like this before."

"That's a point we can both agree upon," said the sheriff.

"And if MTAC hired these guys and put a hit out on my store, you need to round them up as well," said Sam.

"We're already ahead of you there," said the sheriff. "We picked up everyone the three attackers had implicated early on Friday morning. The judge is holding them without bail for now, but none of them are talking."

At school, Jake had just walked Danni to her next class after their second period, math. Walking the halls while holding her hand made everyone fade into obscurity. It felt as if the entire school was empty except for the two of them, and even while taking in T'Aer Bolun Dakkar's detailed telepathic report from the store, Jake was certain that Danni was the most beautiful girl walking the earth.

Somehow she could fill that previously vacant capacity in Jake's mind that had caused his thoughts to wander aimlessly before finding T'Aer Bolun Dakkar and her. The combination of the two of them added gravity to Jake's thoughts. His lightning-fast mind could still handle a plethora of activities simultaneously, but in Danni and T'Aer Bolun Dakkar, he found balance.

After dropping off Danni at her third-period classroom, Jake continued down the hallway to his art class. The teacher had given the class an optional homework assignment over the long weekend that could be used for extra credit. Jake was smiling as he pulled the protective cardboard tube from his shoulder sling and placed it in the pencil tray at the base of his tilted drafting table. Not surprisingly, no one else had completed the homework assignment, having opted to enjoy the long weekend in other ways.

Jake's table was at the very back of the classroom because he'd always been very secretive about his artwork. Mrs. Nelson had always been supportive of Jake and was willing to accommodate his eccentricity to encourage the expression of his artistic abilities.

As she approached Jake's table, he unrolled his drawing and secured the edges to the table with semisticky architect's tape. When she rounded the edge of the table, her eyes grew wide in absolute disbelief. The other students in the classroom noticed Mrs. Nelson was completely mesmerized, seemingly unable to even blink. One by one, they all left their desks and made their way to the back of the classroom. Except for the initial open-mouthed gasp by everyone who viewed Jake's drawing, not a word was spoken, and the entire room fell silent.

On his drafting table was a thirty-six-inch-by-forty-eight-inch drawing of the earth as seen from the upper atmosphere. The detail was maddeningly precise, capturing the curvature of the planet on a clear starlit night, just as the sun crested the easternmost edge of the horizon. Each star in the distance was astronomically correct in its position, and the separation of the wispy clouds between the upper atmosphere and the deep blue of the Atlantic Ocean drew the mind into the perception of a three-dimensional image captured on a large flat sheet of paper.

As they continued to stare, the image seemed to be moving—rotating, if you will—in the direction of the rising sun. The depth, breadth, width, and excruciating detail of the image created the illusion of looking out the window of an orbiting spacecraft down at a planet from miles above it. It was almost as if you could physically reach into the drawing and feel the chill of the extreme outer atmosphere while floating in the void between space and the earth's gravitational pull. No matter how long everyone stared, the emotional grip exuded by the hand-drawn image was relentless, releasing no one from the gravity of its perfect beauty.

With Mrs. Nelson's left arm hugging her waist and her right arm clutching the buttons of her sweater, there were tears streaming down her face. Several of the students were experiencing the same unexplainable rush as they stood transfixed, staring unblinkingly at Jake's drawing.

From far, far away, Mrs. Nelson noticed a faint sound growing louder and more intrusive until she realized the class bell was ringing. They'd spent the entire hour in trancelike silence, nearly motionless while glued to the spot, trying to comprehend with their eyes something to which their hearts had grown immediately and irretrievably connected. Awakening from their hour-long daze, the students groggily gathered their belongings, leaving the classroom in an apparent drunken stupor, intoxicated by the beauty of something impossible to forget yet unbearable in its memory.

Carefully removing the tape and rolling the drawing up into parchment paper before slipping it back inside the protective tube, Jake approached Mrs. Nelson. "This is for you, Mrs. Nelson," he said. "You saw me this way when no one else could, and I am grateful."

"Thank you, Jake," said Mrs. Nelson, her eyes still swollen as she blinked and smiled at him.

"You're welcome, Mrs. Nelson," said Jake, turning to leave the room without looking back.

Outside the classroom, Danni was waiting for him with a bewildered look on her face. "What happened in there, Jake?" she asked. "Why did everyone look so overwhelmed coming out of the classroom?"

"That is the beauty of art," replied Jake. "When it's done well, it can change everything." As they headed down the hallway toward the cafeteria, Jake asked, "What would you say if I told you I had a dragon?"

"I'd believe you," she said. "When can I meet him?"

CHAPTER 25

SAM AND THE sheriff managed to keep the investigation under wraps this time. The only people who officially knew the details of the bungled Thanksgiving Day attack were Sam and the sheriff, the two deputies who'd been on duty at the station that night, and the investigators from the county CSI office. Of course, the three occupants of the semiflattened Yukon knew what they had done, but no one had even suspected that Turbo and Jake knew more about it than everyone else combined.

At the store later that afternoon, Jake sat in Sam's office, completing his homework assignments, while Turbo was curled up under the desk at his feet. Their silent conversation wasn't even remotely related to Jake's homework, but Jake's brilliant mind actually worked at such an efficient level, he could easily contemplate the strategy of exposing MTAC's underhanded transactions while naming the 206 bones in the human body.

"But how can we shut them down?" asked Jake. "They are a huge corporation with money to burn, and as clever as Dad and his crew are, if they continue being attacked, eventually, one of the attacks will get through."

"We don't actually have to take them down. We simply need to change their course. Not everyone working for MTAC is a criminal," said T'Aer Bolun Dakkar. "The majority of MTAC's personnel are simple workers. They are only trying to put food on the table and provide for their families. The laborers have nothing to do with the corporation's policies and most certainly didn't have anything to do with hiring hitmen."

"I know," said Jake. "Some of the people at the Thanksgiving dinner actually work for MTAC and are still struggling to feed their families."

"Which tells you how far they are willing to go just to get their way," explained T'Aer Bolun Dakkar. "Several of their own employees would have been severely injured or even killed if those rockets had made it into the building."

"Which would have given them excellent cover and deniability by allowing them to claim they were also impacted by the attack," added Jake.

"They would have been unwilling martyrs in MTAC's diabolic agenda," said T'Aer Bolun Dakkar. "Undoubtedly, this was a calculated risk by MTAC. The poorest of their employees are those who just signed on with them."

"Yes, and they haven't been working there long enough to receive any of the benefits they were promised," added Jake. "MTAC would get all the sympathy, none of the blame, and they wouldn't even be required to cover the health or life insurance benefits for any of those employees."

"You don't have to capsize an entire ship with everyone aboard it just to prevent it from sailing in the wrong direction," stated T'Aer Bolun Dakkar. "You need only change the captain, for it is ultimately he who will decide the destination of the vessel."

"But how do we find out who the captain is, and how do we get him to change his mind?" asked Jake.

"We do it by making one destination much more appealing than the other," replied T'Aer Bolun Dakkar. "In MTAC's case, we need to make the outcome of their current actions publicly untenable while offering them a solution that leaves room for—"

"An epiphany," said Jake, finishing T'Aer Bolun Dakkar's thought.

"Precisely," agreed T'Aer Bolun Dakkar, impressed by Jake's emotional growth over the past several months.

Finishing the last of his homework, Jake said, "Now all we need to do is find the person whose mind is in need of change, and I am all over that."

Out in the store, people were browsing the collection of Christmas tree ornaments, lights, and other decorations Big Sam's stocked for the holiday season. They'd already sold over one hundred of the donated trees from the lot outside, and with toys, clothing, canned goods, and houseware pouring into Sam-ta's Workshop from all over the state, they were on track to exceed even their most optimistic estimates for the year's charitable donations.

As Jake went about his restocking job, refilling the depleted shelf inventory, Turbo was close behind him as they continued the mental conversation. The speed at which they could communicate in this manner was stunning. Whereas normal people spoke in words and sentences, Jake and T'Aer Bolun Dakkar communicated by exchanging entire ideas in vast detail. In this manner, they could consider thousands of possibilities within the space of an hour without misunderstandings resulting from semantic misinterpretations. In effect, each of them could mentally analyze the pros and cons of an idea while integrating those elements with the highest possible likelihood of succeeding into a single plan shared by both of them.

Since the various stages of the final plan were then known by each of them, down to the last menial detail, the execution of their jointly developed strategy required neither a written itinerary nor a wordy deliberation regarding its execution. Their approach was akin to building a perfect master-planned community without the need for even a single blueprint. By the time Jake had completed his meticulously aligned restocking of the store shelves and finished sweeping the floors in the retail and shop areas, their strategy was nearly a living thing, ready for implementation.

Later that evening, as Jake and Turbo sat in the living room with Samuel and Sarah, Jake asked, "Dad? Mom? Do you think it would be possible for me to visit Madison McClure in Atlanta, Georgia?"

Samuel was very familiar with the name Madison McClure. It was on every letter, press release, purchase offer, and corporate Christmas card MTAC had ever sent to Big Sam's store. In fact, he had often wondered to himself how someone Like Mrs. McClure could continue lending her image and credibility to a corporation with such abhorrent methods and practices.

"I suppose anything is possible, Jake," said Sam. "I guess that would depend on why you want to visit her and whether or not she'd be willing to meet with you."

"If she would be willing to meet with me, would you be willing to take me there to see her?" asked Jake.

"Of course, I would," said Sam without hesitation. "Just tell me when you're ready to go."

Nodding, Jake said, "Thank you, Dad. I'm working on something important for my American agriculture class project, and I'd like for it to mean something more than just another paper to be turned in, graded, and forgotten."

"That's great, Jake," said Sam, looking toward Sarah and adding, "We're very proud of you, son, and you can always count on our support."

"I know, Dad," said Jake. "I'm very proud of both of you too." Getting up from the couch, Jake headed upstairs to his room, with Turbo close on his heels. "Good night, Mom. Good night, Dad. We'll see you in the morning."

Samuel and Sarah also wished Jake and Turbo a good night as they climbed the stairs and disappeared into Jake's room for the night.

Afterward, they sat there on the couch, staring at each other for a moment before Sarah broke the silence, saying, "I wonder where that came from."

"Who knows?" replied Sam, looking up to his right and shaking his head as he considered Sarah's question. "Jake is a brilliant young man, and I'm sure whatever he's working on will be self-evident the moment he reveals it."

"A true Payne," said Sarah, resting her head against Sam's shoulder. "Just like you."

That night, Jake and T'Aer Bolun Dakkar prepared to embark on the longest journey either of them had ever undertaken in a single night. It would also be the most momentous for both of them, and while Samuel and Sarah slept, Jake and T'Aer Bolun Dakkar silently took to the sky.

Looking beyond the horizon to the northwest, they rapidly took on altitude until the North American lower forty-eight gave way to the snow-covered solace of Alaska. Descending into the remote, sparsely populated Yukon–Koyukuk region, Jake felt it for the very first time. It was the tug of familiarity between related dragons, and this time, T'Aer Bolun Dakkar did not resist it.

Flaring out his massive wings, T'Aer Bolun Dakkar floated slowly to the ground, coming to rest silently in the desolate snowy expanse. In every direction, they were surrounded by snow and ice, with no visible traces of life anywhere near them.

Rearing onto his hind feet, with Jake still mounted on his back, T'Aer Bolun Dakkar extended his wings completely out to his sides and remained motionless in the frozen wilderness. Jake realized that since their first encounter, the dragon had grown substantially. His wingspan had increased by nearly ten feet on each side, and he was at least ten feet taller as well.

Suddenly, out of the darkness rumbled a deep majestic voice, piercing their closed mental bubble without even the slightest of difficulty, saying, "T'Aer . . . Bolun . . . Dakkar . . . Welcome."

Uncloaking, separating himself from the snowy starlit background, and towering dominantly above the two of them stood King Tao Min Xiong.

CHAPTER 26

AS THEY STOOD there in the pristine solace of the barren Alaskan landscape, Jake was already taking mental snapshots of the massive dragon lurking over them. T'Aer Bolun Dakkar was no small dragon either; however, Tao Min Xiong was truly gigantic.

Although his wings remained concealed, his enormous height and girth were shocking, even to someone who'd actually flown to the edge of space astride the back of such a being. The long powerful S-curved neck held Tao Min Xiong's head impressively high, and his powerful legs were probably capable of snapping the backbone of a lesser dragon.

What had immediately occurred to Jake was that aside from an approximately 25 percent size difference, T'Aer Bolun Dakkar was nearly identical to Tao Min Xiong. Although the intricate shade patterns of the two dragons' scales were slightly different, their physical proportions were essentially the same, and while Tao Min Xiong's face bore the markings of an era of constant warfare and battlefield confrontations, the family resemblance was acutely obvious.

"Relax, T'Aer Bolun Dakkar," said Tao Min Xiong. "You are eternally welcome here, my son."

Retracting his wings and concealing them along his sides, T'Aer Bolun Dakkar lowered himself onto all four legs. The snow covering the ground was so deep, Jake remained astride T'Aer Bolun Dakkar so as not to sink completely out of sight beneath the ocean of white surrounding them.

"You have both grown since our last encounter," said Tao Min Xiong, acknowledging Jake's presence for the very first time. "He appears quite capable for such a young man."

"He is a wise and tireless warrior," replied T'Aer Bolun Dakkar.

"Yes," replied Tao Min Xiong. "Your recent spirit victory was quite impressive," he added, referring to the dreamscape battle from days before.

"Thank you, Father," replied T'Aer Bolun Dakkar. "Our bond is indeed symbiotic on many levels, and he has fully embraced the knowledge and skills of his ancestors."

"That is evident," replied Tao Min Xiong. "The two of you defeated my most capable avatars in fewer than seven hours." Addressing Jake directly, Tao Min Xiong said, "Leaving the back of your dragon during such a heated battle and creating two independent points of attack while remaining telepathically connected was daring and quite ingenious, I must admit. Had you been catapulted only one hundred feet higher, you would have escaped Earth's gravitational pull and ended up in orbit."

Smiling demurely, Jake replied, "I would never abandon T'Aer Bolun Dakkar, in battle or otherwise. Our bond is stronger than gravity, and I trust him completely."

"Your wisdom exceeds your years, young Jake. How may I be of assistance to you?" asked Tao Min Xiong.

"I ask only that you allow us passage through the territory of King J'Amal Aidin Kondur under your royal seal. Our visit will be brief, and our intentions are honorable," explained Jake.

"When will you require passage?" asked Tao Min Xiong.

"We would fly over the North Pole and into his territory before sunset and then return to North America before sunrise on the Eastern Coast," stated Jake. "We will bring nothing and leave nothing behind. Not even footprints."

Nodding at Jake and T'Aer Bolun Dakkar, Tao Min Xiong said, "Granted. Follow me."

Simultaneously, the two dragons leapt into the sky, deploying their massive wings and accelerating at blinding speed. Following Tao Min Xiong closely, T'Aer Bolun Dakkar matched him beat for beat as they crossed over the globe just south of the North Pole, plunging into the Greenland Sea. They submerged deep below the surface of the icy water, where they approached and entered an underwater opening. Once again heading upward toward the surface, they emerged from the water inside the belly of an uncharted island.

Being that far beneath the surface, they were enveloped by absolute darkness, impossible even for a dragon's exceptional vision to pierce.

Ahead of them, Tao Min Xiong began to glow. The scales along his body began to open, venting light into what appeared to be a massive cavern. Remembering he'd done that before, T'Aer Bolun Dakkar concentrated his energy until he too was glowing.

The light emitted by the two dragons inside the submerged lair was reflected from the walls, ceiling, floor, and the banks surrounding the underwater entrance. Everything was covered in gold. At certain places, the coating was several inches thick, while at others, it was thin enough to flake off under the pressure of Jake's fingertips. After brief consideration, Jake realized the tomb he was standing in was the massive underwater graveyard of generations and generations of dragons.

It immediately became clear to Jake why T'Aer Bolun Dakkar was convinced the remains of his ancestors would most likely never be found. Without a dragon descendant of one laid to rest here, it would be impossible for a human to find this solemn place—let alone reach it—without actually being bonded to a living dragon. Added to that, the flight here was so fast, even Jake's mind couldn't identify a landmark capable of guiding him back to this secluded location.

As he looked around in awe, he noticed T'Aer Bolun Dakkar's reverence to one particular ledge high up inside a massive chimney-like tunnel. Looking upward, Jake noticed there were hundreds of ledges with recesses dug deeply into the solid stone walls. Each ledge was plated with the solidified blood of dragon ancestors. In places, it was many inches thick, having solidified as it flowed over the edge of the shelves, dripping down the walls and onto the floor of the cavern below.

After a few minutes, T'Aer Bolun Dakkar returned to Jake's location, where they were joined by Tao Min Xiong seconds later. In his hand, Tao Min Xiong held two solid gold medallions that bore no markings of any kind. The larger of the two was given to T'Aer Bolun Dakkar, who pressed it into the scales of his upper left arm. Following suit, Jake pressed the smaller of the two medallions into his left arm, where it was literally absorbed into the scales of his organic body armor.

As T'Aer Bolun Dakkar lowered his body to the gold-plated floor of the cave, Jake did also. Gently placing his massive hands upon the shoulders of both of them, Tao Min Xiong gave the two warriors his blessing.

"These will allow you passage into the realm of any dragon king, for they are forged from the blood of the ancestors of all dragon kings. You will be treated with diplomacy by all dragons and dragon kings from this day forward and forevermore," proclaimed Tao Min Xiong. "Now rise and be gone from this sacred place. Your journey is long, and your time is limited, and even I cannot hold the sun from its appointed rounds."

Diving into the dark watery hole at the center of the chamber, T'Aer Bolun Dakkar and Jake swiftly negotiated the path back to the sunken entryway and upward to the surface of the Greenland Sea, where they immediately took to the air. Directly behind them, Tao Min Xiong exited the water, heading back in the direction of Alaska.

Minutes later, T'Aer Bolun Dakkar and Jake crossed into the realm of King J'Amal Aidin Kondur, where they were often alerted to the proximity of nonfamiliar dragons but never challenged. As they quickly surveilled their targeted points of interest from the skies above China, Jake's mind devoured the sights, mentally absorbing everything before they exited the accommodating King J'Amal Aidin Kondur's territory as promised, leaving nothing behind while taking everything they needed with them inside the impenetrable vault of Jake's incredible mind.

As darkness began to cover the beauty of the fading Orient behind them, the sun pursued them relentlessly as they ripped through the skies as fast as T'Aer Bolun Dakkar's wings could carry them. Diving into the Atlantic Ocean midway between the continents of Africa and North America, T'Aer Bolun Dakkar quickly devoured a much-needed herring swarm he had spotted teeming just below the surface.

As they left the ocean on the final leg of their journey, the sun was just beginning to turn the black skies of the United States' Eastern Seaboard to dark gray. Racing into the remaining darkness, they began their descent into the forest behind Jake's house with only minutes to spare.

As T'Aer Bolun Dakkar morphed into the form of Turbo, Jake collected the clothing from his secret hiding spot and quickly dressed.

Turning to rush back through the woods to his backyard, he stopped abruptly. On the ground in front of him, T'Aer Bolun Dakkar had collapsed.

Kneeling beside his exhausted companion, Jake scooped Turbo into his arms and ran with him back to the house as fast as his legs could carry them, saying, "Hang in there, my friend. You carried me around the world last night. I'll carry *you* from here."

Upon reaching the back door, Jake rushed inside the house and up the stairs to his bedroom as quietly as possible. Closing the door behind them and gently laying Turbo on the bed, Jake crawled between the sheets beside him, hugging the little dog close to his chest just as Sam's alarm clock sounded in his parents' bedroom down the hallway.

After a few minutes, Turbo's heart rate began to slow, and his breathing was once again calm and regular as they both fell into a deep, exhausted sleep.

CHAPTER 27

ON FRIDAY MORNING, when Sam knocked on Jake's door to wake him for school, Jake was still drained to the point of exhaustion himself. Turbo didn't even open his eyes and continued sleeping as Sam approached the bed.

"Are you feeling all right, son?" asked Samuel. "You look a little run down."

"Honestly, I was up most of the night and couldn't fall asleep until shortly after I heard your alarm clock," replied Jake. "Is it all right if I stay home and rest today? I'll download all my classwork from the school's website this afternoon so I won't miss anything."

"Sure, son. Do you think your mom should take you to the clinic and have you checked out?" asked Samuel.

"No, sir," replied Jake, adding, "I just got a bit carried away because of the excitement of my agriculture project. Turbo and I wound up spending most of the night researching and collecting data for my presentation to Mrs. McClure."

Realizing how important the project was to Jake, Samuel said, "All right son, but remember, there's no guarantee that she'll agree to meet with you. I just don't want you to feel overly disappointed if she doesn't respond."

"I understand," said Jake, "but I think my presentation would be very superficial if I didn't at least make the effort to speak with her directly."

"That must be one impressive presentation you're working on, son," said Sam. "Just don't let it completely isolate you from your other responsibilities."

"Yes, sir," said Jake, lying down again next to Turbo, who had yet to even budge.

Before closing the door, Samuel added, "Be sure to at least text Danni and let her know what's going on. Women don't like to feel as if they've been left out or that they don't matter, so a word to the wise . . ." Sam let his words trail off as he closed the door behind him.

Jake was texting Danni before Sam had even made it to the bottom of the stairs. The text was simple but heartfelt, saying, "I won't be in class today. Not feeling well but thinking of you."

Seconds later, Danni replied, saying, "Get better soon. I miss you already!"

"Count on it," Jake responded.

"One, two, three, four, five, six, seven . . . Better yet? LOL!" replied Danni.

"Much! Thank you!" Smiling to himself, with the phone still in his hand, Jake drifted back to sleep next to Turbo.

The two of them slept well into the afternoon, and when Jake finally awakened, it was to the sound of rain falling gently outside his bedroom window. Pulling the curtain aside, he peered out across the rain-washed landscape, recalling the images impregnating his mind, captured during their fantastic mission.

As Turbo slept peacefully on the bed, Jake broke the seal on a new sketchbook and selected an array of colored pencils, sharpening each one before placing them in the tray at the bottom of his tilted drafting table. Opening the sketchbook, he folded the cover over the top edge of the table, securing it to the back with architect's drafting tape. With his tools perfectly arranged and his canvas positioned, Jake was ready to begin.

Closing his eyes, he ran both hands across the textured page in front of him, seeing with his hands the pictures locked inside his mind. Taking the first pencil into his hand, he began creating silhouettes of the images with the precision of a master surgeon. Continuing to sketch the contours with his right hand, he took another pencil from the tray, filling in rough details of his visions using his left hand.

After the contours driven by his mental images were successfully executed, he passed the pencil from his left hand to the right one, which continued filling in the rough details initiated by the left hand. Selecting another pencil from the tray without ever opening his eyes, Jake added color and more clearly defined specifics to the three-dimensional image revolving clearly in his mind.

As Jake would finish one level of the drawing using his right hand, he'd take the pencil from his left hand and continue the progress he'd started with it while starting a distinctly new layer with the now empty left hand. This was Jake's process, and with the exception of T'Aer Bolun Dakkar, he'd shared it with absolutely no one.

Even T'Aer Bolun Dakkar found this method to be dizzying to observe, requiring Jake to be both ambidextrous and diplopic, viewing two separate fields of vision while sketching them independently using his left and right hands simultaneously. Using this method, Jake could recreate stunning images with bewildering accuracy at near-incomprehensible speed.

For the rest of the afternoon, Jake remained immersed in his drawings. With the exception of the soup and sandwich Sarah had brought into his room near midafternoon, he continued uninterrupted like a man possessed, creating image after image as he seared through more than a dozen pages of his sketchbook.

"Glorious!" exclaimed T'Aer Bolun Dakkar, who'd been silently observing Jake for the past hour. "Our journey was well worth the effort."

"Thank you," replied Jake. "For everything. I could never have accomplished any of it without you."

"We are an excellent team," stated T'Aer Bolun Dakkar. "Otherwise, Tao Min Xiong would never have allowed us to pursue such an expansive undertaking."

Remembering the seal Tao Min Xiong had placed upon them, Jake reflexively reached for his upper left arm.

"It's still there," said T'Aer Bolun Dakkar. "It will forever be a part of your organic armor and mine."

"Why did he agree so quickly?" asked Jake.

"Tao Min Xiong thinks differently than any of our dragon king forefathers," explained T'Aer Bolun Dakkar. "He can analyze both your stated goal and the likelihood of your success in accomplishing it based solely on your character."

"But how?" asked Jake. "We'd been acquainted only briefly before he granted our request."

"Jake, Tao Min Xiong has known you since your birth," answered T'Aer Bolun Dakkar. "The adventurous dreams of your childhood, the fanciful visions of journeys astride the back of a dragon, and your daring acts of bravery during dreamscape battles were all real."

Jake listened attentively as T'Aer Bolun Dakkar explained the meaning behind his, at times, lucid dreams. The dreams, which began at the age of seven, had always seemed more real than fantasy. Now Jake understood their meaning and the importance of them. He'd been trained and evaluated to test his physical and emotional compatibility to T'Aer Bolun Dakkar. This was truly Jake's destiny.

"The final test was on Thanksgiving night after the event at your father's store," T'Aer Bolun Dakkar continued. "That sensation of hunger you felt made you eat more because your body would require the additional calories for energy during your battle. While you may not recall all of them, you have fought many such battles in preparation for the one we faced that night."

Suddenly, it was all clear to Jake. He could remember every battle, every mental challenge, every test of his character, and every attempt to derail him from the destiny that Tao Min Xiong so desperately wanted for him. Had he failed, Tao Min Xiong would have had no choice but to choose another bond for T'Aer Bolun Dakkar.

"There have been dreamscape battles for as long as there have been bonded dragons and riders," said T'Aer Bolun Dakkar. "Many of them have ended in defeat within seconds, while others have continued for days before a team emerged victorious. In only seven hours, we defeated King Tao Min Xiong's most skilled and deadly avatars. Something no other bonded dragon and warrior have ever accomplished."

Surprisingly, Jake was not at all shocked by this revelation, sensing a deeper, more urgent motive behind the actions of King Tao Min Xiong. "Why now?" inquired Jake. "Why has everything accelerated over the past few months?"

"Because King Tao Min Xiong... is dying," answered T'Aer Bolun Dakkar. "There are fewer than seven years remaining until the end of his reign, at which time I must ascend and claim his throne."

"Which means I have only six years left to prepare," added Jake, finally realizing what T'Aer Bolun Dakkar had indicated to him shortly after their initial encounter. "My destiny is bound to yours."

"Indeed," replied T'Aer Bolun Dakkar. "In the year of your twenty-first summer, you shall ascend with me."

The look on Jake's face was solemn and resolute as he said, "There is something I'd really like to know."

"Anything I can answer for you, I shall," replied the ascendant dragon king.

"I can ride to the outer edges of the atmosphere and into the deepest depths of the sea with you," said Jake. "But I still have to wait until I'm twenty-one before I'm allowed to do the really cool stuff. Who came up with that stupid rule?" asked Jake, grinning as he stood up from his drafting table, and the two of them headed downstairs.

Samuel would be home soon, and it was time for Jake to feed Turbo and set the table for dinner.

CHAPTER 28

IN THE WEEKS that followed their grand journey that had nearly circled the globe, Jake and T'Aer Bolun Dakkar remained relatively close to home. Their twice-weekly fishing trips were to familiar fishing grounds, either in the Atlantic and Pacific Oceans or in the Gulf of Mexico.

During their outings, Jake and T'Aer Bolun Dakkar intensified their training regimen, working on unconventional attack and parry methods and developing strategies that weren't a part of T'Aer Bolun Dakkar's genetic memory. In the next six years, there would eventually be serious adversaries hoping to claim the throne, which was T'Aer Bolun Dakkar's birthright. While they would first have to defeat Tao Min Xiong's avatars, it was only a matter of time before a challenger would arise, and Jake and T'Aer Bolun Dakkar would be ready.

In the meantime, Jake continued his American agriculture project, researching farming and land preservation methods from all over the world and identifying methods to incorporate them into current and future American farming practices. The highlight of Jake's presentation would certainly be the detailed illustrations, all created by Jake's talented hands and brilliant mind. His hope was that he could convince the MTAC board of directors to consider alternative farming practices that could foster harmony between corporate and traditional farmers while ensuring longevity and a stable agricultural market for everyone.

Outside of Jake's bubble, the holiday season was in full swing, and Sam-ta's Workshop was the center of a flurry of activity. The shop was filled to the bursting point with donations from all over the county and state, and with only a week to go before the collection trucks from the distribution center arrived to tally the donations, Big Sam's estimates already exceeded the previous year's totals by nearly 75 percent.

Because of the fanfare surrounding Big Sam's, the national news networks had picked up on the story, bringing in further donations from the surrounding states and even isolated donations from as far away as Europe. With members of Big Sam's crew basically manning the store around the clock, donations were coming in at all times throughout the day and night.

Since the night of the failed but unpublicized attack on the store, the sheriff had deputies posted in the parking lot during the nighttime hours and regular pass-by patrols throughout the day. While the attackers themselves were locked up pending their court dates, the individuals they'd identified as hiring them were out on bail within hours of being rounded up and hauled in.

In any case, whether it was due to the tightened security around Big Sam's during the Christmas season or simply because they wanted to avoid being further implicated, MTAC stepped back into the shadows, maintaining as low a profile as possible to distance themselves from even the appearance of impropriety—no news coverage, no insulting purchase offers, and no unseemly behavior of any kind that could be traced back to them.

The total disappearance from the media made the appearance of the Bentley limousine in Big Sam's parking lot all the more unexpected. While the rear passenger windows were tinted impenetrably black, the license plate bearing the nomenclature MTAC-1 made it unmistakably clear who was paying the store a visit.

Pulling up to the front of the store and stopping, the driver exited the Bentley under the unblinking eye of Big Sam's surveillance system. Having observed the vehicle from the monitors in his office, Big Sam was already at the front door by the time it had come to a halt.

Without a word, the driver walked around to the rear of the limousine and opened the right rear passenger door. Emerging from the back seat was none other than Madison McClure. Walking down the steps, Big Sam extended his hand in her direction, not expecting the enthusiastic response received from the sole heiress to the McClure dynasty.

"You must be Big Sam," she said, warmly shaking Sam's hand. "I'm Madison McClure, and I've heard so much about you," she added with a smile.

Sam was a bit taken aback, his perplexed reaction obvious. He'd never even imagined standing face-to-face with her or anyone else from a corporation he felt was dead set on driving him out of business by any means possible. "Samuel Payne," he answered cordially. "Nice to meet you, Mrs. McClure. What brings you down to our neck of the woods this lovely Saturday morning?"

"Curiosity," she answered, still flashing a smile Sam wasn't yet quite able to gauge. "I received a handwritten letter from a young man named Jacob asking if he could meet with me. He was willing to come all the way to my office in Atlanta for an opportunity to interview me for a school project."

Weeks earlier, Sam had mailed the letter for Jake, not expecting to receive a response from anyone at MTAC, let alone Madison McClure herself. "That young man would be my son, Jake," answered Sam. "He's been researching and working very hard on a presentation he wants very badly for you to be a part of. I told him not to get his hopes up too high in hoping you would respond, but obviously, I was wrong about that."

"Well, I do get a lot of mail but nothing like the letter your son sent me. Even the handwriting is a work of art," said Mrs. McClure, reaching into her Hermes handbag to retrieve the envelope Jake had mailed her.

As she handed the letter to Samuel, he immediately recognized Jake's artwork. The envelope was an actual page from one of his sketchbooks, decorated with uniquely beautiful drawings on both the inside and the outside. The fold itself was created to exacting standards, involving neither the cutting of the paper nor glue to hold it together. It was held shut with red candle wax bearing the historical Payne family seal.

It was obvious Mrs. McClure had exercised exceptional care in opening the envelope so as not to damage it as it was still in pristine condition. Jake had used one of the Bubble Pak envelopes from Big Sam's to send the letter via the parcel service that collected letters and shipments at the store every evening.

"May I open the envelope to read the letter?" asked Samuel, not wanting to assume permission that had not been expressly given.

"You haven't read it yet?" asked Mrs. McClure, shocked at the revelation. "Of course. By all means."

Removing the letter from the envelope, Sam realized just how painstaking a task creating this letter for Mrs. McClure must have been.

While the center of the page was unadorned white paper, the borders were all immaculately decorated with various crops and agricultural products—such as corn, wheat, soybeans, cotton, fruits, and vegetables—and miniaturized farming landscapes from around the globe.

As stated by Mrs. McClure, the handwriting was indeed a work of art. It was composed in neat cursive script, and while the paper was unlined, each line of the letter was absolutely straight, and each word was perfectly spaced, with absolutely no spelling or grammatical errors. The letter read,

> Dear Mrs. McClure,
>
> My name is Jacob, and I am writing this letter with the hope of convincing you to meet with me personally.
>
> I am currently working on a project for my eighth-grade American agriculture class and would be honored by the opportunity to meet with you prior to submitting the final product to my teacher.
>
> As you are a leader in the corporate agriculture arena, I feel your input would be an essential factor in creating an accurate presentation, representative of both corporate and family-owned farming practices.
>
> My father, Samuel, is the owner of Big Sam's Agricultural Supply in Wilson County, Tennessee, and would be willing to travel with me to Atlanta to meet with you at your convenience.
>
> I anxiously await your response and look forward to meeting with you soon.
>
> Sincerely,
> Jacob Isaac Payne

Closing the letter and reinserting it into the envelope, Samuel had to smile. Once again, he'd underestimated Jake's talents and felt a sense of pride not only for the time and effort Jake had invested in this letter but also that his thirteen-year-old son, in only four paragraphs, had motivated one of the country's most influential agriculture figureheads to travel all the way to Big Sam's store just to meet him.

"Well, leave it to Jake to find just the right tone," said Samuel. "Unfortunately, he's not here today, and we're about to close the store, but come on inside, Mrs. McClure. Let me show you around Sam-ta's Workshop while we talk."

Inside, Sam showed a wide-eyed Madison McClure the inner workings of Big Sam's store and the workshop filled with donations for struggling families across the county. Sam explained how the failing agriculture market had been devastating to many family farms, crippling them in their ability to support themselves. While a warehouse full of donations would certainly help, for the most part, these farmers weren't looking for a handout but rather a hand up.

Looking at Big Sam, Mrs. McClure said, "You are not at all the monster my regional foreman made you out to be. Based on his reports, I was expecting to walk into a covert smuggling ring or a group of homeland terrorists trying to wreak havoc on MTAC's interests."

"Nothing could be further from the truth," stated Sam. "We're all about helping and protecting farmers and their livelihood. A lot of these farms go back generations. While feeding America, they've put kids through college and raised scientists, doctors, lawyers, and soldiers, all while keeping the country's grocery stores stocked with quality produce."

"Then why are we always at odds with each other?" asked Mrs. McClure. "We essentially share the same ideology of feeding America while getting paid for the fruits of our labor."

"If I answer that question honestly, you'll see that our ideologies are about as divergent as fire and ice," said Sam. "However, I love my son, and he feels you are an important part of his research. For that reason and that reason only, I am willing to declare a temporary truce with MTAC."

Nodding slowly in acknowledgment, Mrs. McClure said, "Agreed. For Jake's sake. Now where is this wunderkind?"

"Actually, he stayed at home today to work on his project. Would you be able to meet with him tomorrow afternoon?"

"Unfortunately, I'll be leaving early tomorrow morning," replied Mrs. McClure.

"All right," said Sam. "I've got the perfect solution. I'll call my wife and ask her to prepare an extra place setting. You're having dinner with us tonight, and afterward, Jake can interview you for his project."

"I'm not really accustomed to anyone dictating my schedule for me, but for the sake of Jake's project, I'll make an exception for you," replied Mrs. McClure, smiling.

After calling home to inform Sarah and Jake of their unexpected guest, Sam let Jet and Mac know he was leaving for the night. A few minutes later, his truck was headed out of the parking lot, with the MTAC-1 limousine following right behind it.

Upon hearing that Madison McClure was on the way to their house, Jake collected all his documentation. He'd been ready for that meeting since the day he had mailed the letter to her, but he hadn't expected her to make the trip to see him. Nevertheless, he was excited about this spur-of-the-moment opportunity and wanted to make a positive impression.

Jake's room looked nothing like that of an average teenager. It was neat and very nicely arranged, with his drafting table positioned so he could enjoy the view of the rolling meadow outside his bedroom window. His bed was made, and his belongings were neatly stowed in his closet. In short, his room was a reflection of himself. There was no clutter, and everything had a place to which it was returned immediately after use.

There was a chair at his desk for Mrs. McClure to sit and review the presentation, which he had scanned into his notebook PC. Of course, he still had the actual drawings he'd created, but he kept them securely stowed in the bottom drawer of his nightstand.

Looking out his window, Jake saw his dad's truck turning into the driveway, followed by the MTAC limousine. Just as he was about to leave the bedroom and head downstairs, he heard T'Aer Bolun Dakkar's voice in his head, saying a single word.

"Dragoneer!"

CHAPTER 29

"WHAT?" ASKED JAKE excitedly. "Are you sure?"

"Yes," replied T'Aer Bolun Dakkar. "I am quite certain."

"How could we have missed that? I studied everything about Madison McClure, and there is nothing linking her to the dragoneers," said Jake, perplexed.

"Not her," said T'Aer Bolun Dakkar. "It's her driver."

"What should we do? Do you think I should let Dad know?" asked Jake.

"No," replied T'Aer Bolun Dakkar. "You go downstairs and enjoy dinner with your honored guest. I will remain upstairs until you return with Mrs. McClure to make your presentation. I can assure you, your safety and the safety of your family is paramount to me, and I will not let any danger befall you."

"All right," said Jake. "But stay connected with me. If I lose that connection for even a moment, I will abruptly put a halt to everything."

"That will not be necessary, Jake," said T'Aer Bolun Dakkar. "I will remain connected."

Nodding at Turbo, Jake headed down the stairs just as Samuel was parking in the garage and the MTAC limousine was parking in the roundabout in the front of the house. A few seconds later, Samuel came in through the garage door, greeting Sarah and Jake, and then went to the front door to welcome Mrs. McClure, who was standing on the porch, with the driver behind her at the bottom of the steps.

As Samuel and Sarah welcomed Mrs. McClure inside, the driver asked, "When should I return for you, Mrs. McClure?"

Sarah, being Sarah, said, "Nonsense! We always have plenty of room at our table for guests. Please join us for dinner."

"Well played," said Jake to T'Aer Bolun Dakkar. "He was counting on Mom's hospitality to get him into the house."

"Yes," said T'Aer Bolun Dakkar. "He wanted to get inside the house to look around. That was to be expected."

After welcoming Mrs. McClure and her driver inside, Samuel excused himself to go upstairs so he could freshen up and change out of his work clothes. A few minutes later, he returned to the dining room, and everyone took a seat at the table. Because of the interruption of their daily dining routine, aside from Jake, no one had noticed that Turbo wasn't in his customary spot near Jake's chair.

After Samuel blessed the meal, ever the gracious hostess, Sarah served everyone before taking her seat; then everyone began to eat. Where Sam's talents were in his ability to make almost anything with his mechanical and technical skills and Jake could recreate anything he'd ever seen with his masterfully wielded sketch pencils, Sarah was a master chef, having studied culinary arts at Le Cordon Bleu, Paris, before meeting and marrying Samuel.

Accordingly, the meal she had prepared, even on such short notice, was impeccable. By slightly changing the preparation techniques of the meal she'd already planned, Sarah prepared a gourmet meal worthy of royalty. The potatoes she'd planned to serve mashed were instead served baked au gratin with braised beef short ribs in a red wine reduction. The mixed salad was converted to iceberg lettuce wedges sprinkled with freshly cooked bacon bits, California walnuts, and cranberries drizzled in a red wine vinaigrette dressing. The vegetable casserole was replaced by steamed broccoli and cauliflower florets and cooked baby carrot spears served with hollandaise sauce. For dessert, she'd prepared crème brûlée served with wild raspberries.

While there were the typical niceties exchanged during the meal and a few general yet well-mannered questions were asked and answered, Sarah's meals were meant to be enjoyed without the distraction of heavy ideological discussions at the dinner table. For the most part, the conversation was centered around the incredible meal Sarah had prepared with only forty-five minutes' advanced notice.

"I must say, this was the most delicious meal I've ever eaten," said Mrs. McClure. "That includes the five-star gourmet meals I've enjoyed on multiple continents by some of the most renowned chefs in the world."

"Thank you, Mrs. McClure," said Sarah. "I'm glad you enjoyed it."

"Please," answered Mrs. McClure, "call me Madison, and saying I enjoyed it would be an absolute understatement. It was phenomenal."

"Thank you, Madison," replied Sarah. "I really do appreciate that."

As they sipped coffee after the meal, Madison turned to Jake, saying, "If I'm going to promise you my full attention, we'd better get started on our interview."

"Yes, ma'am," said Jake, heading to the stairs leading up to his bedroom. "Right this way."

Following Jake, Madison headed toward the stairs, followed by her driver.

"I'm sorry, but the interview is only for Mrs. McClure," stated Jake, looking directly at the driver.

"Oh, well, I, um . . . Actually, I was only looking for a restroom," stammered the driver unconvincingly.

"It's to the left of the stairs," said Jake, pointing to the door.

Reluctantly, the driver walked over to the restroom and entered it, closing the door behind him as Jake and Madison walked upstairs to Jake's bedroom.

Entering the room, Madison was immediately enamored with the little white Chihuahua sitting on Jake's bed. As she approached him, Turbo tilted his head to the left and then to the right while looking directly at her.

Despite her otherwise haughty demeanor, she couldn't control the urge to extend the back of her hand toward him, saying, "Oh my god! He is so cute!"

Samuel and Sarah had heard that sentence dozens of times over the past eighteen months and were so accustomed to it, they barely even took notice. The driver, who was just reemerging from the bathroom downstairs, was a different story. He realized that the dog Svend Erickson had mentioned to him was upstairs in Jake's room. Although he sat in the living room with Samuel, his curiosity as to what was upstairs in Jake's room noticeably distracted him from the dialogue in which Samuel attempted to engage him.

Upstairs, Jake asked Madison to take a seat, explaining, "My presentation is 100 percent visual. As you watch the slideshow, my artwork should tell the entire story if I've captured and presented everything properly. Afterward, I will ask only one question, if that's all right with you."

"That sounds reasonable," said Madison with a patronizing grin. "Let's begin."

With that, Jake lowered the lights in the room and started the slideshow.

With the very first image, the grin immediately evaporated from her face. It showed an agricultural landscape in China in such vivid detail, it was impossible to look away. Madison's jaw dropped involuntarily as the hand-drawn time-lapsed images showed the evolution of the farm over a thousand-year period. At the conclusion of the first set of drawings, the first and last images were overlaid, showing that over the years, the farm had remained nearly unchanged. The healthy fields and abundant harvest had survived and prospered throughout the entire thousand-year time frame.

Similar presentations depicted farms like the King's Farm in the Faroe Islands from the Kingdom of Denmark, dating back to their origin in the eleventh century, the Matanaka Farm in New Zealand, dating back to the 1840s, the Gorreana Tea Farm in the Azores, established in 1883, sugar cane fields of India dating back to 500 BC, and a number of farms across Europe that had operated continuously for between five hundred to eight hundred years. At the end of each segment, the overlays showed the farms had either maintained or increased their harvest yields despite periods of drought, war, flooding, and wide-scale financial hardship.

The next segment addressed the American agricultural evolution, highlighting farms like the Tuttle Farm in Dover, New Hampshire, and the Shirley Plantation in Charles City, Virginia, both of which had operated continuously since the early 1600s. Once again, the overlays from their origins to their modern-day status showed either persistent or expanded harvest returns while working in harmony with the environment to ensure ecological balance.

The next segment of the presentation was dedicated to corporate farming entities like the Middle Tennessee Agricultural Corporation or MTAC. The look on Madison's face was clearly distraught as she watched farm after farm—either purchased, annexed, or acquired via hostile takeover—producing abundant harvests at the point of their acquisition and quickly deteriorating over a period of less than a decade. The overlays showed how these farms had dramatically withered and declined under MTAC's management, often producing nothing but stunted crops, barely suitable for feeding to livestock.

The final segment showed the farmers and families behind the agricultural success stories. Their farms were successful because those people putting in the work felt a connection to them. They valued the importance of working with Mother Nature to ensure the longevity and health of their farms, associating their farm's success with the success of protecting and preserving Mother Earth by applying eco-friendly farming practices.

The segment concluded with the families devastated by the greed and callousness of companies like MTAC, whose only concern was their immediate bottom line. These families had invested generations in working and preserving the land, producing abundant harvests year after year by applying sound farming practices like crop rotation, erosion control, natural soil conditioning, and biologically produced fertilization. Within ten years, farms dating back to the early days of American colonization had withered away to nearly nothing under MTAC's ownership.

The sullen faces of these lifelong farmers were painfully captured in Jake's depictions. The tear-streaked faces of women who'd supported their husbands as they worked the land to provide for their families, only to lose everything to the soulless MTAC entity, were dramatically depicted in Jake's compelling drawings.

The emotional impact of Jake's images weighed upon Madison McClure's conscience like an anvil as she sat there, glued to the screen, with tears streaming down her face. As the screen slowly faded to black, she sat there sobbing, feeling the pain of those hardworking people whose lives had been bought and destroyed by the board of directors she'd entrusted with the daily management of her company. She felt that she had personally harmed these people by her lack of involvement. As she sat there, gasping for breath between sobs, her heart was breaking as she wondered, *How could I have been so blind . . . so foolish?*

Turning to Jake, her voice audibly cracking as she attempted to wipe her tear-filled eyes, she said, "This is all my fault. This is all because of my lack of concern. I was so blinded by dollar signs, I hadn't considered the lives we were destroying. This is horrible. This is not who I am, Jake. Honestly." She openly wept, remembering the images seared into her memory like a brand mark.

"May I ask my question now?" asked Jake.

"Yes," said Madison nearly inaudibly.

"Will you help us fix this?" asked Jake.

Looking at Jake, Madison answered, "I have to. I could never forgive myself if I didn't, and I really mean that."

Standing beside her chair, Jake handed her a flash drive containing the presentation she'd watched with him. "This is for you," he said. "There are also a few suggestions included on the drive that could be of use in charting a new direction."

"Thank you, Jake," said Madison. "I promise you, there will be some major changes when I get back to Atlanta." After composing herself, she stood and walked toward the door. Looking back, she added, "You are a remarkable young man, Jake. I'm glad I was able to meet you."

"One more thing," said Jake, handing her another picture. "The man who drove you here is not who he claims to be."

Looking down at the sketch, she saw it was a perfect likeness of the driver from MTAC who'd picked her up at the airport.

"Who is he?" asked Madison.

"I'm not sure, but he was arrested back before Thanksgiving. I saw the arrest on the news and recognized his face as soon as I saw him at the door this evening," said Jake.

"I'll tell him he can go when I get downstairs, and I'll get another ride back to the hotel tonight. If you think he's dangerous, I believe you." As Madison opened the door to leave the room, she noticed there was no one downstairs in the living room. Making her way down the stairs, she called out, "Sarah? Sam?"

There was no answer. At the bottom of the stairs, she saw Sarah and Sam sitting in the dining room. Sam was looking at her, shaking his head ever so slightly, trying to warn her.

Slowly walking toward them, she felt a faint rush of wind pass by her just as she saw her driver in the corner. He was holding a handgun pointed toward Sam and Sarah as he stood near the door leading out onto the back porch.

"Come in here and take a seat, Madison," said the driver. As she walked slowly into the dining room, the driver told Sam, "Call your son down and tell him to bring the dog with him."

There was no way in hell Sam was going to call Jake down and put him in danger. He was considering how many rounds he could absorb before breaking this idiot's neck when suddenly, the back door opened and the driver was literally snatched out the door into the dark backyard.

Sam immediately leapt up from the table, rushing toward the back door and flinging it open. The backyard was empty. The driver had literally vanished into thin air.

CHAPTER 30

SAMUEL AND SARAH stood with Madison on the back porch, looking out into the empty yard. Sam had reached the door only a few seconds after the driver was snatched through it, but with the exception of a light breeze blowing through the trees at the edge of the forest, absolutely nothing was moving. The driver had been so forcefully snatched out the door, he'd dropped the handgun he'd been pointing at Sam and Sarah.

In the roundabout near the front door of the house, T'Aer Bolun Dakkar held the driver securely wrapped inside his wings, depriving him of oxygen. After a few seconds in the dragon's embrace, his struggling diminished and then stopped completely as he lost consciousness and went limp. When T'Aer Bolun Dakkar reopened his wings, the driver fell into Jake's waiting arms.

Jake caught the unconscious man and lifted him easily, placing him back inside the limousine at the driver's seat. Using the key fob inside the man's pocket, he hit the panic button, setting off the car alarm and attracting Samuel's attention.

Samuel bolted around the house to the front yard, with Sarah and Madison following cautiously behind him. T'Aer Bolun Dakkar held onto Jake and leapt silently into the air and over the top of the house, quietly landing in the backyard, where they slipped back inside the house and up the stairs to Jake's room.

In front of the house, Samuel rushed up to the limousine, where he discovered the driver in the front seat, slumped over the steering wheel. Madison was already on her mobile phone with the 911 operator when Samuel opened the car door. As the man began to regain consciousness, he opened his eyes just in time to see Samuel's anvil-sized fist closing in on him, sending him back into his oblivious slumber.

Sarah rushed into the house through the front door, screaming, "Jake! Where are you, baby?" while racing toward the living room.

At the top of the stairs, Jake, with Turbo, emerged from his bedroom, asking, "Is everything all right, Mom?"

Realizing they were both safe, Sarah ran up the stairs, taking her son in her arms, hugging him closely to her, while Turbo poked his head through the stair rails, barking at nothing but feeling as if it were the appropriate thing to do at the moment.

Outside, Madison was on the porch, where she remained on the phone with the emergency operator pending their arrival. Samuel was standing beside the limousine, watching over the driver, hoping he would open his eyes again and try to escape.

When he did open them again, the sheriff and two deputies were there to welcome him into the cold reality of being handcuffed and placed under arrest. Another deputy was inside, taking statements from Sarah and Madison, while Jake and Turbo remained upstairs in Jake's bedroom.

Out near the gate at the edge of the property line, a news crew who'd picked up the radio transmissions on a police scanner was recording the scene with zoomed camera lenses. Some of the neighbors, reacting to the sirens and police lights, had made their way down to the gate as well, curious as to what was going on.

Thanks to the prominently displayed vanity plate on the limousine, it was clear to everyone that MTAC was involved in some form or another; however, no one out there knew the exact nature of that involvement.

The first sheriff's vehicle to leave the property transported the limousine driver, who was in the back seat with his head covered in an attempt to remain anonymous. The sheriff's tow truck followed them with the limousine they'd taken as evidence. After taking statements from Sam, Sarah, and Madison, the sheriff's deputies also left the house, heading back to the station, where they would process all the information they'd received.

The sheriff, who'd remained behind after all the other deputies departed, turned to Big Sam and asked, "Do you have any idea what your surveillance videos are going to show us this time?"

"I honestly have no idea," said Sam. "Obviously, the camera from the stair landing will show what happened in the living room and part of the dining room, and the exterior cameras covering the house should show how the man got from the back door to the limousine, but honestly speaking, I don't know what to expect."

"Lately, I don't either, Sam," said the sheriff. "Mrs. McClure's statement seems to match your and Sarah's statements, so MTAC's involvement is unclear. Perhaps the cameras were able to catch enough to fill in the blanks for us."

"I honestly don't believe Mrs. McClure was involved in any of her driver's actions. She seemed as shocked as the rest of us when she saw him with the gun," said Sam. "Besides, whatever sucked him out the back door was so fast, none of us could believe our own eyes."

"All of you claim he was asking for Jake and his dog, but what could he have possibly wanted from them?" asked the sheriff.

"That's where my well runs dry, Sheriff," replied Sam. "Jake's a good kid, and he never lies to me or anyone else. His dog is cute as all get out, but I can't imagine someone being willing to shoot us over Turbo."

Looking at Sam, the sheriff got into his cruiser, saying, "There are still a lot of puzzle pieces missing here. Hopefully, we'll be able to get something out of the driver that'll help us explain some of this stuff."

"Well," said Sam, "I'll leave that part of the puzzle up to your investigators, but I'll certainly be here if you have any questions for me."

"Good enough," said the sheriff, waving as he headed back down the long driveway.

Inside, Sarah and Madison were in the living room, sipping coffee, trying to make sense of all that had transpired. Suddenly, Madison's eyes lit up as she remembered the sketch Jake had given her. It had totally slipped her mind until Sam walked into the room. Reaching into her handbag, she withdrew the folded page Jake had given her just before she left his room.

Opening it and laying it on the table, she said, "Jake gave me this before I came downstairs. He told me I should be careful because he didn't think my driver was who he claimed to be."

Picking up the sketch, Sam's eyes widened. It was unmistakably the limousine driver. "How did he get this, I wonder?"

"He didn't say," said Madison.

Looking up the stairs toward Jake's door, Sam called out, "Hey, Jake, come down here for a minute, son!"

Upstairs, Jake opened the door and headed downstairs, with Turbo close at his heels. In the living room, Jake said, "Yes, sir?" as he stood there, sheepishly looking down at the floor with his hands behind his back.

"Madison told us you gave her this picture of her driver. Where have you seen him before?" asked Sam.

"A few places," said Jake. "He's been in the store a couple of times, mostly when it was really busy. He was also at the park, watching me and Turbo, and once, I saw him driving by when I was walking to the store after school."

"Why didn't you say anything?" asked Samuel.

"I never saw him doing anything threatening, and I didn't ever feel like I was in danger," said Jake. "Then I saw him on the news with that man who showed up here the Sunday after the store was broken into."

"You mean that Svend Erickson guy?" asked Sam.

"Yes, that's the one. I've seen him with a few different people hanging around the store and across the street at Belle's Diner, next to the gas station," answered Jake. "I didn't say anything because sometimes people think I'm just imagining it when I see things that they don't."

"Well, this certainly wasn't a figment of anyone's imagination," said Sam. "What about the others? Did you sketch pictures of them too?"

"Yes, sir," said Jake, revealing the sketches he'd been holding behind his back and handing them to his father.

"You're right, Jake. I've seen a couple of these guys too," said Sam. "In fact, I'd seen them even before I saw them getting arrested on the news with that Mr. Erickson character. I just didn't pay them the attention that you did. Obviously, I should have."

"I sketch everything that seems new or odd or out of place, but you have a lot more to keep an eye on," said Jake. "It's only natural that some things would slip by you unnoticed."

"You're quite an astute young man, Jake," said Madison, clearly amazed at the depth of his character.

"Thank you, Mrs. McClure," said Jake, adding, "I'm sorry your visit turned out like this, but I'm very glad you took time to meet with me and listen to my presentation."

"The pleasure was all mine," said Madison. "You and your family are the most hospitable and kind people I've met in a very long time, and I will be making some major staffing changes on Monday when I'm back in Atlanta."

"Speaking of which," said Samuel, "you are more than welcome to stay here in the guest room tonight, and I'll drive you to the airport tomorrow morning after breakfast."

Standing, Madison said, "It does sound tempting, but I really do need to get back to my hotel tonight. I've got a lot to go over and several phone calls to make before Monday morning."

"Well, the least I can do is drive you back to your hotel," Samuel volunteered, grabbing his keys. "Would you mind getting Mrs. McClure's coat from the closet?" he asked, looking at Jake.

Without a word, Jake retrieved Mrs. McClure's coat from the closet near the front door and helped her into it. Afterward, he followed her and Samuel into the garage, opening and holding the door for her as she climbed into Sam's truck.

"Thank you, Jake," said Mrs. McClure. "I will be in touch with you soon."

Jake nodded in response, and he, Sarah, and Turbo watched and waved as Sam backed out of the garage and headed down the lane with Mrs. McClure.

"She is not what I expected at all," said Sarah. "I must say I was pleasantly surprised."

"I was too," said Jake. "Even Turbo liked her."

"I'm not sure why her driver was so fixated on you and Turbo, but I want you two to stay close to the house for the next few days," said Sarah. "If you're not at school or at the store with your dad, I'd rather you stay close to home, at least until after the Christmas and New Year's break."

"Yes, ma'am," said Jake, nodding. "I'll use that time to finish the presentation for my American agriculture class. Except for when I take Turbo out, I'll be at home anyway."

"I just want to make sure you are safe, Jake. If something were to happen to you, I don't know what I'd do," said Sarah.

"I know, Mom. I promise I'll be careful, so don't worry," Jake replied. "I'm not a little boy anymore. After all, I recognized those guys were trouble before anyone else did."

Looking at Jake, Sarah realized for the first time that her son really *was* growing up quickly and had already become quite an amazing young man. "I know," said Sarah. "But I'm your mother, and it's my job to worry about you for the rest of my life. Just don't go growing up too fast on me, young man."

"I understand, Mom. You've been there watching over me my entire life, and I'll love you for that forever," answered Jake, adding, "But I also want *you* to know if the need ever arises, you can also count on *me* to protect you."

Sarah smiled as she watched Jake and Turbo head up the stairs to his room again, thinking, *We've done well, Samuel Earle Payne . . . very well indeed.*

Madison spent most of the time on her mobile phone during the ride back to her hotel. Whoever she was talking to on the other end was certainly getting an earful as she fully exercised the power of her position. In the time it took for Sam to get her to the hotel, she'd fired the local foreman who hired the driver without looking into his background, set up a meeting for Monday morning with the executives from her board of directors in Atlanta, and informed her personal secretary to have the heads of every regional office present at that Monday morning meeting. As Sam pulled up to the covered passenger drop-off point at the front of her hotel, she reflexively reached into her handbag for her wallet.

"Unless you're hell-bent on offending me, you'd better be reaching into that bag for your room keycard," said Samuel matter-of-factly.

Still looking down, she stopped rummaging through her handbag and smiled. As the doorman opened the door for her, she looked at

Samuel and said, "You're a good man, Big Sam, and you have my word. From now on, you will have zero problems with MTAC. I personally guarantee it."

"I believe you," said Sam, extending his hand to her. "Thank you."

"It is I who thank you," she said, firmly shaking his hand. "Give my best to your amazing wife, and tell Jake I'll be in touch. I'd like to fly all of you out to Atlanta after the New Year so Jake can make his presentation to my department heads." Looking Sam directly in the eye, she added, "We can do better. We *must* do better."

"Good night, Mrs. McClure," said Sam as she exited the truck and the doorman closed the door behind her.

At the steps, she paused briefly to wave at Sam, her mobile phone already pressed against her ear again as she disappeared into the hotel lobby.

CHAPTER 31

MADISON MCCLURE WASTED no time in tackling the corruption problems inside her organization. Within twenty-four hours, news of the corporate shake-up at MTAC was dominating headlines all over the country.

Before her flight back to Atlanta, she gave a press conference in the lobby of the hotel announcing sweeping changes in the leadership structure of MTAC. Furthermore, investigations had been initiated to determine the extent of the fraud perpetrated by MTAC in the hostile takeover of family farms all over the state.

By the time Monday morning had rolled around, half of the MTAC board of directors were shaking in their boots, wondering if they'd still be employed by the end of the day or walking out of the building in handcuffs. As they filed nervously into the boardroom, no one said a word as they all stared blankly at their notepads and briefcases on the table in front of them. There was no small talk or self-congratulating back pats. Everyone just sat there, wondering what would come next.

At nine o'clock sharp, Mrs. McClure walked into the boardroom, placing her designer leather satchel on the table, saying, "You are about to watch an agricultural presentation made by a teenager, an eighth-grader from Wilson County, Tennessee."

At the far end of the table, one of the self-absorbed corporate vice presidents audibly scoffed at the notion of wasting his time, sitting through the school project of some pimply faced kid.

Without even looking at him, Madison pushed the intercom button for the personnel office, saying, "Miranda."

"Yes, Mrs. McClure?" came the immediate response.

"Prepare a termination package for Alan Blankenship, three-month salary limit, accrued vacation and sick day compensation, immediate credentials cancellation, and security-escorted removal from the property," Madison said, ending the call without waiting for a response from Miranda.

Thirty seconds later, two security guards were at the door of the boardroom to remove Mr. Blankenship from the building.

"You can pick up your check at the welcome desk before you leave the property, Alan. As I was saying," Madison continued, "you are about to watch a presentation by a student named Jacob Isaac Payne. He's invested a lot of time in putting this together, so I'd like you to give it your undivided attention." Looking around the boardroom, she added, "If you don't feel you can silently and objectively view this half-hour presentation without interruptions, speak now, and you can collect your check at the welcome desk along with Mr. Blankenship."

No one moved. No one else scoffed. No one rolled their eyes, and not a single word was spoken as Madison scanned the room for additional would-be hecklers. Lowering the lights with the remote built into her chair, she started the presentation.

As had happened with Madison while watching the presentation, everyone in the boardroom was immediately enthralled by the dramatically detailed images. A sense of mass hypnosis seemed to settle over everyone in the boardroom, including Madison, who had already watched the presentation at least a dozen times.

At the conclusion of the presentation, Madison slowly brought up the lights, revealing the sullen, tear-filled eyes of every single person in the room. The sense of guilt hammering them was as thick as fog among the nineteen remaining corporate directors who sat there, speechless.

As Jake had done after she had first watched the presentation, Madison asked a single question. "Will you help me fix this?"

"Yes," said Melissa Chambers.

"Yes," answered Michael Worley.

"Yes," replied Marcus Williams, Timothy Aldean, Sylvia Newton, Martin Baker, Terrance Oliver, Jason Benson, and every other corporate director in that boardroom as one by one, they committed to Jake's cause.

Madison stood up and walked around the boardroom conference table, stopping to place a copy of the flash drive on the table in front of every chair, including the one left empty by Alan Blankenship, just to drive home her commitment to making this a priority, even over the objections of long-term employees like Mr. Blankenship.

"Christmas is one week from today," stated Mrs. McClure. "I need you all to review the suggestions accompanying the presentation on your flash drives and submit your ideas for implementation of them to me by Friday."

Looking around the boardroom, Madison could see the impact of Jake's presentation on this room full of millionaires whose fortunes had been built on the suffering of hardworking farmers and their families.

"We've got a lot to make up for," she said. "Let's get to it."

Two hundred fifty miles away, in Wilson County, Jake and Danni sat across from each other in the school lunchroom, discussing what had happened on Saturday at Jake's house. The rumor mill at the school was running rampant with all sorts of wild theories and totally unfounded assumptions; however, Jake and Danni were all but oblivious to them as they sat there, enjoying their lunch together.

"You mean she actually came to visit you?" asked Danni excitedly. "That is so cool!"

"Yes, and she told Dad she would fly my whole family to Atlanta to meet with her corporate executives," answered Jake.

"Is she hot?" asked Danni, smiling.

"I wouldn't know," said Jake. "Looking at you is like staring into the sun. After that, everything else sort of pales in comparison."

Danni seemed pleased by Jake's answer as she smiled, looking down and poking at the remaining fries on her lunch tray. "Jake, you say the sweetest things to me," she said.

"I only tell you the truth," said Jake. "The thing is the truth *is* sweet when it comes to you."

"Can I ask you something?" asked Danni.

"Of course," replied Jake.

"A couple of weeks ago, you asked if I'd believe you if you told me you had a dragon." Pausing and leaning closer to him, she whispered, "*Do* you have a dragon?"

In his mind, Jake heard T'Aer Bolun Dakkar saying, "It's all right, Jake. You can trust her. She will never betray us."

"Yes," replied Jake, whispering, "I do have a dragon."

"Can I meet him?" asked Danni.

"You already have," replied Jake. "You just didn't know it at the time."

"Really?" asked Danni, obviously excited. "What does he look like?"

Reaching into his backpack, Jake withdrew one of his ever-present sketchbooks titled "Dragons." Opening it to the first page, he showed Danni the very first picture he'd drawn of T'Aer Bolun Dakkar. In the pages that followed, he revealed more detailed drawings of the dragon, which were incredibly lifelike, seeming to come alive on the pages as she reviewed the pictures in awe.

"These are amazing, Jake," she said, continuing to flip through the pages of his sketchbook. Halfway through the sketchbook, she paused to ask, "How did this picture of Turbo get mixed in with the rest of your dragon pictures?"

As she looked up at Jake, waiting for the answer to this curious question, Jake was looking at her with a smile on his face. Suddenly, she realized what he was showing her, and her eyes opened widely as her jaw dropped.

"Oh my god!" said Danni, whispering excitedly. "Turbo *is* your dragon!"

Jake didn't need to say another word because the smile on his face and the look in his eyes as he raised his eyebrows said everything. Closing the sketchbook, he slipped it into the cellophane cover and put it back inside his backpack.

"You know I want to meet him," said Danni, looking around as if scanning the room for eavesdroppers. "I promise not to tell anyone."

"I know," said Jake. "Turbo told me I could trust you, and he's got great intuition when it comes to things like that."

"This is so exciting!" Danni squeaked, and for the remainder of their lunch, she asked every question she could think of, never even considering the fact that Jake could either be insane or lying to her. As

Jake walked her to her last class of the day, she asked him, "Can I *please* meet him sometime? Please, please, pretty please?"

Smiling, Jake nodded, saying, "Give me a few days to figure it out, and I'll formally introduce you to each other. He's anxious to know you better as well."

Smiling from ear to ear, Danni put her arms around Jake's neck, tiptoeing as she kissed him on the cheek, curling her left leg up behind her. Jake smiled as they parted, darting off to their respective classes before the final bell rang.

As Jake reached his classroom seconds before the bell, he heard T'Aer Bolun Dakkar in his mind saying, "I have a plan I think you'll approve of. I'll tell you about it at the store after school."

Jake was a thousand miles away as he sat through his American agriculture class. While everyone else was working on their presentations, which would constitute one-third of their midterm grade, Jake had already completed his and instead opened his backpack to remove one of his many sketchbooks. Selecting the colored pencils required to create his masterpiece, he went to work on a different project: his Christmas gift for Danni.

CHAPTER 32

TWO DAYS BEFORE Christmas, two big rigs pulling forty-foot container trailers were parked outside Sam-ta's Workshop. As Big Sam watched the donations being loaded into them, he had to smile, remembering the times when all the donations received would fit easily into the bed of his pickup truck. Now he was signing sheets and sheets of inventory forms, releasing hundreds of thousands of dollars in merchandise to the drivers from the charitable organization who would distribute the goods to those in need of them.

In the few days since Madison McClure's visit, MTAC had completely disappeared from the news coverage, and all judgments and claims against family-owned and operated farms had been halted. Even the cavalry of MTAC pickup trucks, which were so commonplace on the dirt back roads connecting farms all over Wilson County, had basically evaporated into thin air. There was a genuine sense of hope and relief as the impact of Mrs. McClure's course realignment gained traction across the state.

The department heads from the corporate office in Atlanta had actually been contacting local farmers who'd been hit hard by MTAC's illicit tactics. Now they were extending olive branches to those farmers and seeking paths to reconciliation that would return the land and the dignity to those families who had lost so much and suffered for so long under the cruelty of MTAC's management policies.

For families either unable or unwilling to reclaim their farms because of the length of time that had passed or the difficulty involved in reestablishing farms that had been neglected to the point of total loss, MTAC issued checks to cover the huge gap between the true value of their land and the embarrassingly low prices they'd been hammered into accepting.

All these things were only the first steps in the corporate rebranding efforts undertaken by MTAC, but for the families impacted by the billion-dollar intervention, it was indeed a godsend.

Later that afternoon, as Sam and Turbo wandered through the wide-open multilevel warehouse, making sure nothing was inadvertently left behind, Sam's cell phone rang, echoing loudly in the empty chamber. Looking down at the call screen, Sam saw that it was Mrs. McClure calling.

"Mrs. McClure," answered Sam, smiling. "Merry Christmas to you."

"And to you," replied Madison. "I hope I'm not interrupting anything."

"Oh no. Not at all," said Sam. "The trucks just left with all the donations we collected, so Turbo and I were walking around the warehouse to make sure nothing was overlooked."

"From what I hear, that was quite a haul," said Madison, genuinely happy for Big Sam.

"Indeed, it was," answered Sam. "So what can I do for you on this lovely afternoon?"

"Listen, I know Christmas Eve is tomorrow, but I'd like to fly you all to Atlanta in the morning," said Madison. "I want to introduce your family to my board of directors, and we have something we'd like to formally present to Jake."

"Well, I'm not really used to having my schedule dictated to me, but since it's for Jake, I'll make an exception for you," Sam chided, channeling her words from their first meeting.

"Touché!" she said, chuckling. "Anyway, I promise to have you back home by tomorrow evening."

"We'll be there," said Sam. "I'll book the flights and get you the details by this evening."

"No need. I'll be sending my Gulfstream for you," she said. "I'm sure Jake would enjoy flying on something so fast and unique."

"Well, if you insist," said Sam.

"I do," said Madison. "I'll send a driver to pick you all up and get you to the executive airport."

"Hmmm," said Sam jokingly. "My experience with *your* drivers hasn't been among the most comforting things I've done lately."

"Point taken," said Madison. "But I'll be sending my personal chauffeur this time. She's been with me for eighteen years, and you can trust her beyond all doubt."

"Sounds good," said Sam. "We'll be ready, and we'll see you tomorrow morning."

As it was the last day of school before the holiday break, students were released at 1:30 p.m., so Samuel sent everyone home early and closed up shop for the year. Afterward, he and Turbo headed over to the school to pick up Jake. Outside the school, Jake and Danni were holding hands, walking up to the curb near the parents' pickup and drop-off point.

Turning to look at her, Jake said, "I have something for you, Danni."

"Really?" said Danni, clearly excited.

Sliding the cardboard poster tube off his shoulder, he handed it to her, saying, "It's a Christmas present, so don't open it before Christmas morning."

"Oh! That's not fair," she said. "You know how much I love your artwork. Waiting that long is going to be torture for me."

"Good things come to those who wait," replied Jake, smiling at her. Still looking into her eyes, with his back to the cars approaching behind them, Jake, apparently out of nowhere, said, "Turbo just told me you're cute when you laugh."

"Really? How did he—"

"Hey, Jake!" Sam called out from the pickup lane.

Peeking over his shoulder, Danni saw Samuel and Turbo looking at them through the passenger side window of the truck.

Leaning forward, Jake whispered into her ear, "He's a dragon. You'd be surprised at what he can do." After kissing her on the cheek, Jake turned and headed off toward his dad's truck. Looking back over his shoulder, he reminded Danni, "Don't open it until Christmas morning."

Julia Hawthorne pulled up to the curb just as Jake was getting into Sam's truck, waving at them as Danni climbed into the car. "Merry Christmas, you guys!" she said. "Give Sarah our best!"

"Yes, ma'am. Merry Christmas to you too," said Jake as he and Sam waved to her out the lowered window before exiting the school parking lot.

Inside the truck, Sam asked Jake, "Are you and Turbo up for an early morning flight?"

For an instant, Jake's heart skipped a beat, thinking Sam was onto them.

Before he could overreact, T'Aer Bolun Dakkar telepathically told him, "It's not that kind of flight, Jake."

"Sure," said Jake. "Where are we going?"

"Madison McClure wants to fly us all to Atlanta in the morning. Evidently, your presentation has created enormous waves in the upper echelons of MTAC," explained Sam, leaving out the part about them formally recognizing Jake's work.

"*Seriously?*" asked Jake, obviously excited about the trip.

"She called less than an hour ago, and I just got the thumbs up from your mom," said Samuel with a big grin on his face. "She's even sending her personal chauffeur to pick us up and her private jet to fly us there and back."

"That sounds great!" exclaimed Jake.

In his mind, he heard T'Aer Bolun Dakkar asking, "Are we going to ride in one of those slow-moving little metal tubes with wings?"

"Apparently," answered Jake telepathically.

"I could have us all there in minutes," said T'Aer Bolun Dakkar blithely.

"But *you* don't serve refreshments," replied Jake.

"True," agreed T'Aer Bolun Dakkar. "Well, it should be an interesting experience, to say the very least."

As Jake closed his eyes and leaned back in the seat, his thoughts were on the Christmas gift he'd given Danni. He could have drawn her from memory long before their first meeting at the Harvest Festival. Since that day, he'd locked every aspect of her into his airtight memory, creating a mental image of not only what she looked like but also how he saw her.

For Christmas, Jake had given Danni . . . herself. He'd given her a view of herself as seen through his eyes. He'd captured her smile and her laughter and the way she'd peek from beneath her bangs when she was embarrassed. He'd given her the sunshine in her hair, the freckles on her nose, and the excitement in her eyes whenever she saw him walking toward her.

It wasn't a beautiful picture; it was an *accurate* picture of a girl Jake found beautiful. It captured her from a perspective most people would never see of themselves, showing her strengths and her vulnerabilities along with the joyful nature that clearly separated her from everyone around her.

The picture was not a collage but rather an assortment of her many facets. There would be elements of it she would find silly and wonder why he'd included them and other elements she would find stunning, nearly forgetting that *she* was herself, that stunning girl.

Having completed it the night before giving it to her, he'd spent nearly as long on this single piece of art as he had on his entire American agriculture presentation. In typical Jake fashion, the picture possessed a quality that would literally draw the viewer into it. After only a few seconds, the details seemed to take on multidimensional characteristics in the image's overall appearance, giving it a sense of motion, even while remaining static.

Despite it being his own handiwork, Jake sat mesmerized in front of his drafting table, staring at the collection of images that seemed to come alive within the boundaries of his artistic canvas. By the time he was able to pull himself away from the enchanted image, the gray light of dawn had already begun filtering in through his bedroom window.

"She'll love it," said T'Aer Bolun Dakkar inside the realm of Jake's astonishing mind. "She'll love it because she loves you."

CHAPTER 33

THERE WAS ONE sketchbook Jake had never taken with him to school or anywhere else, for that matter. It had never left his room and remained locked in the bottom drawer of his nightstand. For his trip to Atlanta, Jake made an exception to his normal rule and took it with him for the meeting with Madison McClure.

The limousine arrived shortly after 7:00 a.m., collecting an excited Jake along with his entire family, including Turbo. The forty-minute trip to the executive airport was predictably uneventful as the seasoned driver dispatched by Madison McClure skillfully navigated the near-empty streets to MTAC's private hangar, where her private jet was fueled and ready for takeoff.

Mrs. McClure had accounted for everything, including the in-flight breakfast served the moment the aircraft reached cruising altitude. While it was no match for Sarah's big Sunday morning breakfast, it was certainly a cut above anything Jake's parents had ever eaten on a commercial flight before. She'd also arranged for an in-flight presentation introducing the MTAC staff and department heads and briefly explaining the responsibilities of each of them.

While Jake and his parents attentively watched the video presentation, Turbo was glued to one of the aircraft's tiny windows, watching the clouds pass slowly by and counting the dozens of other aircraft creeping across the morning sky. While the flight seemed exceptionally short to Samuel and Sarah, Turbo felt as if they were nearly marking time, barely moving forward at all.

Jake was indifferent to the speed of the flight, concentrating on the MTAC video and the key individuals being introduced. By the time the aircraft had landed in Atlanta two hours later and taxied into the private hangar, Sam and Sarah were impressed, Turbo was impatient and ready to get out of the archaic flying machine, and Jake was well prepared, having memorized the full presentation, including the names and faces of the entire board of directors.

A limousine nearly identical to the one that had picked them up earlier that morning was waiting inside the hangar, ready to take them directly to MTAC's headquarters inside the McClure International office building in the heart of Atlanta. Having flown with them from Nashville, Mrs. McClure's driver once again efficiently navigated the semivacant city streets, safely delivering Jake and his family to the private underground parking garage below the building.

After parking the vehicle, the driver ushered her passengers to the elevator only a few steps away from the reserved parking spot. Looking around the parking garage, Sam noticed there were several limousines and luxury vehicles in the garage bearing license plates from Georgia as well as the surrounding states.

"Looks like it's going to be a full house," stated Sam. "There's got to be close to a billion dollars' worth of vehicles parked down here."

"You should see the private collection Madison inherited from Wilbur McClure," said the driver as she pushed one of only two buttons on the elevator panel.

"I'd love to," answered Sam.

"It's one level below the presidential suite. I'd be happy to give you all the guided tour after your meeting if you'd like."

"What do you think, Jake?" asked Sam. "Should we check it out?"

"Absolutely," replied Jake, looking at the driver. "Thank you, Ms. Richardson."

Looking curiously at Jake, the driver asked, "How do you know my name?"

"You're in the presentation we watched during the flight," answered Jake. "Ms. Denise Richardson, senior transportation supervisor."

Nodding approvingly, Ms. Richardson stepped to the side as the elevator slowed and came to a stop. When the doors opened, Jake and his family were met by the applause of several dozen smiling men and women lining the walkway to a glass-enclosed conference room. Their applause wasn't forced or insincere but rather accompanied by the warmth of true appreciation. Walking toward them from the conference room with a broad smile on her face was Madison McClure, also applauding Jake.

"Welcome to McClure International!" she said. "We're so glad you could make it."

After hugging Sarah and shaking Sam's and Jake's hands, she guided them all into the enclosed glass box overlooking downtown Atlanta, Georgia. While they took a moment to absorb the view from the upper floors, the remaining directors made their way into the conference room, taking their designated seats at the long polished wooden table.

Seats were reserved for Jake, Samuel, and Sarah near Madison's chair at the head of the table. As they settled in, Turbo took a spot on the floor near Jake's feet. Once everyone was seated, Madison removed the integrated remote control from the arm of her director's chair and stood to address the board of directors.

"Ladies and gentlemen, first of all, I'd like to formally welcome our esteemed guest, Jacob Isaac Payne, and his parents, Samuel and Sarah," she said, adding, "Oh, and Turbo, who's sitting here on the floor near Jake."

Nearly everyone seated at the table took a moment to peek underneath it to recognize Turbo astutely sitting there.

After a few seconds, Madison called the room to order, saying, "Over the past decade, McClure International has been a leader in international corporate agriculture. However, in recent years, our profits have declined, leading us to adopt more aggressive means of meeting our production quotas. Unfortunately, as a company, we stopped seeing the big picture and became so narrowly focused on those declining profits that we were unable to see the most important element of the entire agricultural process—the farmers."

After Madison pushed a button on the remote she held, the windows of the boardroom darkened, becoming completely opaque. With the push of another button, the wall behind her illuminated from within, becoming a large high-definition viewing screen.

Continuing, she explained, "By eliminating the farmers from our business model, we thought it would be a simple matter of automating the process in much the same way the automotive industry has done, reducing the number of actual human beings required to complete the process, thereby reducing the cost of production."

As everyone watched the wall behind her, Jake's hand-drawn images filled the screen, illustrating the dramatic decline in the yield volume of farms previously managed by caring families. With each year, the production of farms under the corporate management of MTAC showed constant declines, even as they were forced to pour more and more money into those farms in an effort to stem their losses.

Samuel and Sarah sat speechless, viewing the images their son had so meticulously created, images so emotionally powerful, they had swayed the policies of one of the world's largest agricultural corporations.

"Thanks to you, Jacob Isaac Payne, MTAC has embarked on a new era of cooperation with the most important element of agricultural success," said Madison. "Those farmers who are up before dawn, investing love and sweat into the success of their farms and bringing the fruits of their labor to a market that literally feeds the world."

As she explained MTAC's new business philosophy, Jake's beautiful images continued to reinforce the importance of the change MTAC's board of directors had now wholeheartedly embraced.

"We believe it is our responsibility to not only work the land but also revere it. While we cannot undo the mistakes of the past, we can and must avoid making those same mistakes in the future, placing profit over the lives of those who give their farms the one element money cannot buy—love," stated Madison.

At the conclusion of the presentation, Mrs. McClure turned off the viewing screen and slowly reduced the window shading, allowing natural light to once again flood into the room.

"Each year," continued Madison, "McClure International recognizes the individual within our organization who has, through their actions and personal engagement, most positively affected the organization's business trajectory and improved the lives of both our corporate family and those we thankfully serve with our products and services throughout the year." Looking around the room at the approving smiles of her staff, Madison announced, "This year, it is our great honor to recognize Jacob

Isaac Payne as the recipient of McClure International's Agricultural Innovation Award. Congratulations, Jake!"

Around the table, spontaneous applause erupted as all the meeting attendees rose to their feet, joining Madison in acknowledging Jake's achievement. Jake's parents were speechless as one by one, all the board members passed by Jake in turn, shaking his hand and congratulating him along with Samuel and Sarah for raising such an outstanding young man. The last person in the long line was Madison McClure.

"It is my pleasure to present you, the recipient of the award, with this certificate of achievement along with an all-expense-paid vacation package for you and your family to the U.S. Virgin Islands anytime within the next twelve months," said Mrs. McClure, adding, "and, lastly, a check for one million dollars."

Jake's eyes widened, and his jaw dropped in utter disbelief. Never in his wildest dreams would he have imagined he could affect such a change, and he was humbled beyond description by this award. "Thank you, Mrs. McClure and everyone else here," said Jake. "This is truly amazing."

"You've earned this, Jake, and it is all of us here who have you to thank for reminding us of my father's original vision for the company," said Mrs. McClure, adding, "By the way, we're also picking up the taxes on that check for you."

After a few minutes of congratulations and Merry Christmas wishes, the meeting was adjourned, and people began filing out of the room toward the elevators.

Seizing that moment of opportunity, Jake approached Mrs. McClure, asking, "Can I talk to you in private? I have an important message for you."

Although a bit taken aback by Jake's question, Madison knew that it was important for her to hear what Jake had to tell her. After asking Denise to show Sam and Sarah the car collection on the floor above them and assuring them she and Jake would join them in a few minutes, she invited Jake and Turbo into her private office, adjacent to the boardroom.

Once inside her office, Jake removed one of the sketchbooks from his backpack, placing it on the desk in front of him. The title on the cover was "Ghosts." Opening it to the final drawing, he slid the sketchbook over to Mrs. McClure.

Tears immediately erupted from her widened eyes as she covered her open mouth with her hand, gasping. There on the desktop was the unmistakable image of her father as she had last seen him before he died of a massive coronary infarction. In the image, he was flashing the smile he always wore whenever he saw his "Little Maddie."

Catching her breath, she looked up at Jake, asking, "How did you know?"

"He's been with you for a very long time, trying to draw your attention to the way people were corrupting the corporation and tarnishing his legacy," said Jake. "He was with you in several of the images I found on the internet while I was searching for you."

"But how?" asked Madison. "I never mentioned him to you."

"When I was researching the MTAC properties around Wilson County, he approached me," said Jake. "He told me how much it hurt him to see the way family farmers were being treated by the MTAC foreman and his staff in Tennessee. He expressed to me just how corrupt they had become and appealed to me to contact you."

Madison was openly weeping as she listened to Jake while staring at her dad's picture. "I'm so sorry, Daddy." She sobbed. "Please forgive me."

"He says, 'There is nothing to forgive, Maddie,'" Jake offered. "He doesn't blame you at all."

Suddenly looking up at Jake, Madison asked, "How did you know that's what he called me? Is he here now?"

"Yes," replied Jake. "He was also with you when you came to our house in Tennessee. He stood behind you with his hand on your shoulder while you watched the presentation in my room."

"I felt him there," said Madison. "I felt his disappointment, and it broke my heart that his legacy was being distorted into something awful."

"You were feeling his pain," said Jake. "You are his only heir, and there was no one else he could turn to. It was so frustrating for him that it was binding him to this plane and preventing him from moving on."

"Oh, Daddy. I'm so sorry. I didn't know," said Madison as she continued to weep.

"He hears you," said Jake. "Would you like to see him?"

Pausing momentarily, she looked at Jake and asked, "Can you do that? Can you help me see him?"

Reaching across the desk, Jake said, "Take my hand."

As Madison placed her hand in Jake's, she closed her eyes and heard her dad's voice to her right, saying, "Hi."

Turning in his direction, she opened her eyes to see him standing next to her, smiling.

"Hey, Maddie. I love you, baby girl," her father said to her. "You did good, kiddo, and I'm very proud of you."

"I love you too, Daddy," said Madison as she stared at her father with loving adoration. "We're going to fix everything. I promise. We're going to make everything right."

"I already know that, Maddie," he replied. "I just wanted you to know I believe in you and to help you find the right path before I moved on. I'm ready. Now I can rest." Turning to look at Jake, Mr. McClure said, "Thank you, Jake. I am eternally grateful for your help." Turning back to his daughter, he said, "I love you, Maddie, and I will be watching over you always."

Smiling at her, his image began to glow brightly before dissipating into the room and finally vanishing completely.

Before releasing Jake's hand, Mrs. McClure squeezed it tightly, telling him, "Thank you, Jake. Thank you so very much."

After a moment, Madison disappeared into the bathroom in her office. While she was gone, Jake carefully removed the sketch of her father along the perforation at the top of the page and left it on the desk for her. When she returned, she was once again the consummate professional, beaming with a previously unseen happiness and self-assurance that most certainly would have made her father proud.

After leaving the office with Jake and Turbo, the three of them joined Sam and Sarah in the showroom upstairs, filled with hundreds of millions of dollars' worth of collectible automobiles, none of which were even a fraction as valuable as the last "I love you" she was able to share with her father.

CHAPTER 34

AFTER TREATING JAKE and his family to a gourmet lunch in the company's very own five-star restaurant, Madison made sure they were back at the airport in plenty of time to make it home by late afternoon.

During the flight back to Tennessee, Jake asked his parents, "Mom, Dad, what should I do with all the money they gave me?"

"It's your money, Jake," said Sarah, smiling. "You can do whatever you'd like to with it."

"And they didn't give it to you. You earned it," Sam added.

"Can I give it to you and Mom?" asked Jake. "I'm not sure what to do with this much money."

Looking at each other, Sarah and Samuel smiled together before Sarah answered, "No, Jake. Your father and I have been abundantly blessed over the years, not least of all by you. When and if your dad ever decides to, we can retire quite comfortably."

"After Christmas, I'll go to the bank with you, and we can open an account in your name," said Samuel. "If you let it work for you and accrue interest over the next few years, you can build the type of financial security that will allow you to choose your own path in life."

"That sounds reasonable," said Jake, turning to look out the window with Turbo.

T'Aer Bolun Dakkar had been silent for most of the trip, observing and remaining ever watchful while Jake and his parents enjoyed their brief but exciting journey to Atlanta. Using his direct line of communication with Jake, he said, "I don't see how people can fly in these things. It takes so long to get anywhere."

Smiling, Jake answered, "Consider it an adventure or a slight change of pace."

"A 'slight' change of pace?" said T'Aer Bolun Dakkar. "We could have flown to Tahiti and recharged our armor in the time it takes this device to make it home from Atlanta."

"Not everyone has the benefit of being bonded to a dragon king," said Jake with a smile. "Besides, you're hungry and impatient right now because we couldn't go fishing last night."

"As always, your words ring true," answered T'Aer Bolun Dakkar.

A few minutes later, they began their descent into Nashville, accompanied by scattered snow flurries from an overcast gray sky. By the time Denise safely dropped them off at their front door, those flurries had stabilized into a steady snowfall that would most certainly continue through the night.

"You're welcome to stay with us and stick out the snowstorm, Ms. Richardson," Sarah offered.

"I appreciate your hospitality, Mrs. Payne, but I'm looking forward to getting back and spending Christmas with my fiancé and his family. Besides, once we're in the air, the rest of the trip will be a breeze," said Denise, smiling.

"Well, Merry Christmas to you and your family, and congratulations to you and your fiancé," said Sarah, waving as Denise got back into the limousine and headed down the lane.

"She'll be fine," said T'Aer Bolun Dakkar to Jake. "The brunt of the storm won't reach Nashville until they're in the air and well on their way back to Atlanta."

"That's good," said Jake, comforted by T'Aer Bolun Dakkar's flawless weather predictions.

Inside, the Payne household was fully prepared for Christmas. The tree had been trimmed and decorated since the day after Thanksgiving, and the abundance of presents beneath it had everyone excited and anxious to open them on Christmas morning.

While the day itself had not been unusually long, the excitement and travel involved resulted in an early bedtime for everyone. By 10:30 p.m., Samuel and Sarah were sound asleep, and by 11:00 p.m., T'Aer Bolun Dakkar and Jake were splashing into the frigid waters of the

North Atlantic, where the dragon finally ate his fill of the herring he'd been so desperately craving.

Sure enough, in the time it took for them to fly from Nashville to Atlanta in the Gulfstream, Jake and T'Aer Bolun Dakkar had flown to the Atlantic Ocean, devoured an enormous swarm of herring, and were already landing silently in the woods behind the house.

Later, after they crawled back into bed upstairs, Jake asked T'Aer Bolun Dakkar, "Is it odd that I was more excited about MTAC's recognition of my efforts than I was about the money that came with it?"

"Not at all," replied T'Aer Bolun Dakkar. "You created something utterly amazing without even knowing you'd be rewarded for it. The research and artistic effort you invested in your project came from a place much more meaningful than the superficial quest for riches and notoriety."

"My sentiments exactly," said Jake. "Just knowing I could create something that would motivate others to stop and reconsider their decisions was the only motivation that really mattered to me."

"King Tao Min Xiong showed great wisdom in choosing you, Jake. You are truly a noble man, both in your thoughts *and* your actions," stated T'Aer Bolun Dakkar. "Besides, you are already incalculably wealthy."

"What do you mean?" asked Jake.

"The seal Tao Min Xiong placed upon us was not a temporary permit. It is a royal decree identifying his chosen ascendants."

"But his reign will last another six years," stated Jake.

"True. However, while we may not yet question his royal mandates or issue mandates of our own, you have already passed his evaluation of your ethics and honesty. Therefore, the royal lair and all the riches within are as much ours now as they will be upon Tao Min Xiong's passing."

"But I've never faced any sort of honesty or ethics challenges from King Tao Min Xiong!" exclaimed Jake.

"The true test of honesty does not come with the announcement that you are being evaluated but rather at a moment when you can choose wrong over right without personal consequence," explained T'Aer

Bolun Dakkar. "Inside the lair of our ancestors, you were purposely left unattended, surrounded by the gold of a thousand generations of dragons. Most men would not have been able to resist the temptation of taking at least *some* of it. Had you done so, you'd have been free to take as much as you could carry, but you'd never have received King Tao Min Xiong's blessing or his royal seal, and our bond would have been dissolved the moment you returned home."

"I had no idea," said Jake, remembering his time inside the lair. "The thought of taking anything from that sacred place never even occurred to me."

"Which is precisely why King Tao Min Xiong has chosen you as my bonded ascendant. Even when tempted by the gold of a thousand generations, you remained steadfast in your integrity and unwavering in your desire to accomplish the difficult task ahead of you," T'Aer Bolun Dakkar explained. "There is no greater test of will than that of a man's hunger for gold. By taking none of it, you now possess all of it."

"What an odd paradox," said Jake. "Giving someone more of something because he didn't want any of it in the first place."

"It is simply proof that you will always choose honor and truth over riches and notoriety," stated T'Aer Bolun Dakkar, "and that solitary decision has made you the wealthiest man to ever walk the earth."

Shaking his head in absolute disbelief, Jake said to T'Aer Bolun Dakkar, "Earlier today, I was wondering what to do with a check for a million dollars. Now I discover I own an underground cavern filled with a billion tons of pure gold."

"It has indeed been an eventful day," said T'Aer Bolun Dakkar. "I'd suggest we sleep on it."

Jake was already way ahead of his dragon, having fallen asleep seconds earlier, wondering what Danni would think of the present he'd given her for Christmas.

CHAPTER 35

THE SOUND OF Jake's phone buzzing on the nightstand woke him early on Christmas morning.

It was an incoming text from Danni that read, "Are you awake yet?"

The sky outside was still gray as Jake peered out the window over the landscape completely blanketed in snow. Rubbing his eyes, he responded to Danni's text with a simple "Yes," and ten seconds later, his phone was ringing.

Answering it, Jake said, "Merry Christmas, Danni Hawthorne."

Completely skipping the salutatory platitudes, Danni sailed right into her emotional reaction. "I love it, Jake! This is the most amazing present I've ever gotten! It is so unbelievably beautiful. There are no words to describe the way it makes me feel. I've been staring at it since midnight, and I can hardly take my eyes off it for even a second. There are so many different elements and elements within those elements and details that are simply amazing. Oh my god, Jake! Do you really see me this way? It's so incredible. I just love it! I just love . . . you."

Feeling as if she'd run past the goal post, Danni stopped talking, hoping she hadn't blurted out too much with that last declaration.

Finally hearing a pause long enough for him to squeeze in a response, Jake said, "I love you too, Danni, and I am happy because *you* are happy."

Clearly relieved yet still very excited, Danni said, "I got you something too. I hid it at the bottom of the zipper pocket on the side of your backpack. It's nowhere near as special as the gift you gave me, but—"

"Don't say another word," Jake interrupted. "This is perfect."

The moment she had mentioned where she'd hidden her gift, Jake grabbed his backpack and scooped everything out of the zippered pocket. At the very bottom of it was a small narrow box wrapped in velvety red paper crowned by a small golden bow. He frantically opened it to find a golden men's bracelet. On the outward-facing side were the words "Jake & Danni," and on the inward facing side were the words "Danni & Jake."

"I'm already wearing it," said Jake, beaming. "It is truly wonderful."

"I have one too!" said Danni. "It's the girl's bracelet, of course, but the inscription is the same, only on opposite sides."

"It is the most precious gift I've ever received, and I will never take it off," said Jake.

"I have to go for now," said Danni in an emotional flurry of words. "Everyone else is downstairs opening presents, but I wanted to call you first before I join them. Merry Christmas, Jake. You are amazing, and I'll text you later today."

"Thank you, Danni, and Merry Christmas," answered Jake as the call ended.

Slipping on his house shoes, Jake headed downstairs to the living room, with Turbo close behind him.

Sam and Sarah were already at the kitchen counter, sipping coffee, and as Jake and Turbo walked toward them, they simultaneously exclaimed, "Merry Christmas!"

"Merry Christmas, Mom and Dad," Jake responded, looking at all the presents spread out beneath the Christmas tree.

"Well, let's get to it, sleepyhead," said Sam. "Those presents aren't going to open themselves."

Excitedly, everyone sat on the floor, looking through the boxes in search of those bearing their names. For Sarah, there was a diamond-encrusted heart-shaped pendant and an amazing pair of Italian designer riding boots from Sam.

Sarah had given Sam a beautiful wool-lined men's overcoat she'd ordered from one of the vendors at the Harvest Festival. Dangling from one of the buttons was a golden chain that disappeared into the coat's watch pocket. Withdrawing the chain, Sam discovered an intricately detailed Cartier pocket watch. It was something he'd always wanted but would never have purchased for himself.

Jake had saved up all the money he'd earned working at the store just for Christmas. Realizing his dad was totally a gadget guy, Jake had purchased a high-tech remote-controlled drone for Samuel. It had a full forty-five-minute flight duration and could be launched remotely from its charging base and piloted from anywhere in the world as long as there was cellular service or a high-speed Wi-Fi connection. Best of all, it would automatically return to the charging station whenever the battery was low, preventing it from crashing or being lost.

For Sarah, Jake had ordered a thirty-six-piece cookware set, something she'd been meaning to get for years but never seemed to have gotten around to. It was all made of heavy-duty stainless steel with thick copper bottoms. Although Jake had no idea what some of the pieces were used for, Sarah most definitely knew and was absolutely thrilled with it. According to her, it was something she'd wanted since the day she had graduated from the culinary academy in Paris, France.

For Turbo, Sam and Sarah had given him an assortment of extra-large rawhide chew bones. As tiny as he was, they were amazed at how quickly he could chew through the ones intended for small dogs, and although these bones were larger than Turbo, he happily grabbed the largest one in the assortment and headed over to his day bed in the corner to start destroying it.

For Jake, Sam and Sarah had purchased an amazing Polychromos pencil set containing 120 pencils of varying colors and shades. Up to now, he'd been creating masterpieces using a set of fifty pencils they'd purchased for him from the dollar store years ago. The new pencils were accompanied by the highest-quality drawing paper Jake had ever seen, and he couldn't wait to use it. Now he had all the tools necessary to help him take his artwork to the next level. Walking over to Sam and Sarah, Jake put his arms around both of them at the same time, hugging them tightly and thanking them for the amazing gifts they'd given him.

As he stood up to go back over to his coveted art supplies, Sam said, "Hey, son."

Turning to look back, Jake noticed Sam was holding up a keyring with two keys dangling from it. Both Sam and Sarah were smiling as Jake walked back toward them.

Handing him the keys, Sam said, "I believe Santa may have left something in the garage for you."

Taking the keys from his dad, Jake slowly walked over to the door leading out to the garage. Opening it, he was expecting to see Sam's truck parked there. Instead, there was a brand-new ATV sitting squarely in the center of the garage wrapped with a giant red ribbon and topped with a bright green bow.

"Merry Christmas, Jake," came Sarah's voice from behind him.

He turned to find both Sam and Sarah standing there, smiling at him.

"You're a young man now, Jake," said Sam. "It's time you had a young man's transportation."

Fighting to hold back tears of joy, Jake walked toward them once again, wrapping his arms around both of them, saying, "Thank you so much, Mom and Dad. This is amazing, and I love both of you more than you could possibly imagine."

Breaking the silence, Sarah asked, "How about I fix us all some breakfast, and afterward, you boys and Turbo can take it out for a spin to see how it handles in the snow?"

Passing behind them, Jake noticed, Turbo was already dragging another huge rawhide bone from beneath the tree over to his day bed in the corner.

"You've got to try these things, Jake! They're delicious!" said T'Aer Bolun Dakkar.

"You're not supposed to eat . . ." started Jake before dropping the issue in midsentence. Instead, he simply smiled to himself, saying, "Merry Christmas, Turbo."

After breakfast, Sam, Jake, and Turbo headed out to the garage to check out Jake's new ATV. Two years ago, this thing would probably have seemed daunting to Jake, but now he was anxious to try it out.

Following a brief orientation and demonstration by Sam, he handed over the keys to Jake, who immediately mastered its operation. A few minutes later, he was cutting through the snow-covered meadows surrounding the house like a pro.

Satisfied that Jake was more than capable of handling the ATV, Samuel helped him mount a carrier basket to the rack behind the driver's seat. Anxious to experience it for himself, Turbo hopped into the basket the instant they'd finished mounting it.

Before they headed out of the garage, Sam said, "Now remember, Jake. You can use the dirt back roads and trailer paths between farms, but you're not allowed to ride an ATV on public roads and highways, and always be polite and get permission before assuming it's all right to ride across someone else's property."

"Yes, sir," replied Jake, nodding at Sam, who was holding up his mobile phone as a reminder for Jake to call if anything happened.

A few seconds later, they were headed out of the garage and across the meadow outside Jake's bedroom window. Despite the fact that T'Aer Bolun Dakkar could fly faster than anything created by humans, riding the ATV with Jake proved to be more entertaining than he'd imagined it would be. There was something about zipping along, facing into the wind with his tongue hanging out that immediately struck a chord with him.

While Jake would always drive carefully when subject to the scrutinizing eyes of Sam and Sarah, once they were out of eyeshot, Jake and Turbo would cut loose, pushing the ATV to the limit. By pressing his paws against Jake's back, Turbo could interlock them with Jake's armor in precisely the same way they could when Jake was in flight with T'Aer Bolun Dakkar. Using this method, nothing could dislodge Turbo from Jake and the ATV short of Turbo's desire for it to be so.

As an added benefit, Turbo was the ultimate safety enhancement, and on one occasion where Jake had overestimated the ATV's turning capability, causing it to tip and potentially roll over, T'Aer Bolun Dakkar simply deployed his wings, righting the vehicle immediately and preventing the potential mishap.

While Jake had absolutely no idea he'd be getting an ATV for Christmas, Turbo, who had spent most of the time with Sam while Jake was in school, knew exactly what was coming. With a bit of mental navigation along his genetically inherited maps, T'Aer Bolun Dakkar was able to plot a course that would allow Jake to reach Danni's house using dirt back roads without ever having to travel along public roadways.

"Would you like to visit Danni?" asked T'Aer Bolun Dakkar. "I can show you how to get there."

"Absolutely," replied Jake, obviously excited. "Let me text her first though. I'd hate to interrupt them on Christmas morning without asking first."

Pulling over, Jake texted Danni, asking if he and Turbo could come by for a brief visit. It took less than a minute for her to say yes, and shortly afterward, they were on the way to her house.

Her eyes lit up the moment she saw them outside the gate at the end of the driveway. After buzzing them in from the hallway intercom panel, she skipped to the front door and waited under the overhang in front of the house as Jake parked and turned off the engine.

Removing his helmet, he said, "Merry Christmas, Danni."

"Merry Christmas, Jake," she responded, rushing up and hugging him tightly.

"I think you've met Turbo," said Jake, with a broad smile lighting up his face.

"Hi, Turbo!" she said excitedly. "I'm glad you two stopped by to visit."

From behind her, Mrs. Hawthorne said, "It's not polite to make your guests wait outside, Danni. Bring them inside for some warm milk and cookies."

"Thank you, Mrs. Hawthorne, and Merry Christmas to you."

"Merry Christmas to you too, Jake," said Mrs. Hawthorne. "It's very nice to see you again, and Danni just can't stop talking about you."

Rolling her eyes and blushing slightly, Danni said, "Oh, Mom, do you have to tell everything?"

"Well, it's true," said Mrs. Hawthorne. "Besides, Jake is a very nice young man, and I'm sure he's happy to hear that you speak of him so highly."

"Thank you, Mrs. Hawthorne," replied Jake politely.

As Danni, Jake, and Turbo sat near the fireplace in the living room, Mrs. Hawthorne disappeared into the kitchen to prepare the milk and cookies for them.

Looking at Jake, Danni asked, "Is it all right if I hold him to take a closer look?"

Before Jake could even answer, Turbo sprang onto Danni's lap, placing his tiny paws against her chest and staring into her eyes.

Turning to look at Jake, T'Aer Bolun Dakkar asked, "Would you ask her if I can communicate with her telepathically? I can't do it without her permission."

"He wants to know if he can speak with you telepathically," Jake said quietly. "He can't do it unless he has your permission."

"Of course," whispered Danni excitedly.

In her mind, she heard T'Aer Bolun Dakkar's warm, comforting voice saying, "It is an honor to finally meet you, Danni, and yes, Jake also talks about *you* all the time."

Looking at Jake with eyes wide as saucers, Danni said, "This is so cool!"

"What's so cool?" asked Mrs. Hawthorne, walking back into the room, carrying a tray of snacks for everyone.

"Um, this is the first time Turbo has ever let me hold him," said Danni, smiling.

"He is beautiful," said Mrs. Hawthorne, adding, "Speaking of beautiful, the landscape drawings you created are hanging in the lobby at the hotel, Jake, and guests just can't stop talking about them. Every time I walk through the lobby, I find myself stopping to stare at them over and over."

"Thank you, Mrs. Hawthorne. I'm glad you like them," said Jake.

"They are amazing," said Mrs. Hawthorne, adding, "but the picture you gave Danni for Christmas is unquestionably the most fascinating and beautiful work of art I've ever seen. We must have spent close to an hour just gazing at it when she showed it to us earlier this morning."

"Thanks again, Mrs. Hawthorne. I'm glad you enjoyed it," replied Jake as she set down the tray and left the room with a smile.

In the meantime, T'Aer Bolun Dakkar and Danni were locked deeply in conversation, rapidly exchanging ideas and learning about each other.

By the end of their silent discussion, Danni was delighted, and T'Aer Bolun Dakkar said to Jake, "She's perfect."

After finishing their warm milk and cookies, Jake thanked Mrs. Hawthorne for the hospitality, explaining they had to get back home but promising to visit again soon. Danni escorted them out to Jake's new ATV, hugging him again and kissing him on the cheek.

As Jake and Turbo hopped aboard to head home, Danni asked, "Have I ever mentioned that I have the most amazing boyfriend in the whole wide world?"

"You have now," answered Jake, winking at her before heading back out the driveway on their way home.

Twenty minutes later, Jake was pulling up to his house, and when he and Turbo walked in through the garage entrance, Sam and Sarah were stretched out on the couch, watching television.

"How was it?" asked Sam.

"It was absolutely amazing," said Jake, adding, "Thank you, Mom and Dad. I love you both very much" before heading upstairs to his bedroom.

Inside the room, T'Aer Bolun Dakkar said, "You know they were pacing the floor the entire time you were gone, right?"

"Of course," said Jake.

CHAPTER 36

TEENAGERS SPEND A lot of time wishing they could be older, not realizing that those years they are wishing away will slip by faster than they can ever imagine.

With Jake, that was especially true. Understanding the timetable they were up against, he and T'Aer Bolun Dakkar had significantly intensified their training regimen. As a result, both of them had grown noticeably larger and stronger, a detail not lost on Sam and Sarah. By Jake's sixteenth birthday, he was nearly as tall as Big Sam, and because of his ceaseless appetite for knowledge, he'd graduated from high school a full two years earlier than he normally would have.

He'd never touched any of the money in his savings account, opting to learn the valuable life lessons only hard work and dedication could bring. All the while, his account balance continued to grow, as did the volumes of knowledge he'd acquired from his parents and from T'Aer Bolun Dakkar.

After being accepted by Vanderbilt University, Jake immersed himself by majoring in both the anthropology and computer science graduate programs while minoring in art and psychology. Although most people would find it overwhelming to take on majors and minors with such broad yet unrelated curricula, Jake found the challenge invigorating and graduated summa cum laude. At the insistence of Sarah, Jake continued his formal education, receiving both his master of arts *and* master of science degrees shortly before his twenty-first birthday.

For Jake, preparing himself for the mantle of responsibility hurdling toward him was the driving force behind everything he did. While dragons were exceptionally capable when it came to remaining undetected, they were just as vulnerable to environmental changes as humans were. Therefore, it was essential that bonded dragon riders represented the interests of dragons to preserve them as a species.

Historically, dragon riders had been highly educated individuals, often working in positions of power or influence. Their primary mandate was to maintain environmental balance. Since they were even more dependent on nature's bounty than humans were, dragons were akin to canaries in a coal mine. Changes that would be detrimental to humans over time often posed an immediate threat to dragons that must be addressed without bureaucratic delays. Since humans often made decisions and undertook endeavors that were against their own survival interests, bonded dragon riders had often been the barrier that prevented mankind from its own self-destruction.

Jake's seemingly unorthodox combination of educational interests had enhanced his ability to identify the social and psychological motivation behind the actions of different cultures. In understanding their differing perspectives, he could develop practical solutions to problems based on modern scientific research and ensure the accelerated implementation of those solutions across the board using modern cutting-edge technology.

T'Aer Bolun Dakkar had left a lasting impression on Danni during their meeting that delightful Christmas morning. The history and images he'd shared with her were so intensely vivid, she decided right then and there to become a marine biologist. He'd shown her how the oceans were the very cradle of life on Earth and our last hope of saving the planet for generations to come.

For centuries, herring had been a staple food for dragons because of the massive numbers of them and their relatively fast reproductive rates. Now fleets of trawlers had decimated those numbers, plundering the oceans' bounty and reducing their reproductive rates by more than half. While a hungry dragon could consume almost anything, prior to mankind's massive intervention, there were "plenty of fish in the sea," a phrase that was no longer supported by the environmental evidence.

In an instant, Danni had made it her life's mission to prevent the senseless plundering of oceanic life and the unconscionable disruption of Earth's most vital ecosystem. Through intense self-study and private research, Danni had given herself a running start and was accepted at the University of Miami's marine biology department immediately upon graduating from high school.

Living so close to the ocean also came with the added benefit that she could spend lots of time with Jake and T'Aer Bolun Dakkar. It was during her first semester in Miami that they had taken her on her first dragon flight. As she was sitting astride T'Aer Bolun Dakkar's neck, with Jake directly behind her, holding her securely in place, they took to the air early one morning, traveling down the coast to Key Largo to watch the sunrise.

After spending the day soaking up sunshine and the evening enjoying the view from a beautiful beachfront restaurant, they left, flying back up the coast under a canopy of dazzling stars. While they didn't risk flying too high or too fast, the pure exhilaration of flying with Jake astride T'Aer Bolun Dakkar was the most intoxicating experience of Danni's entire life. Afterward, she was more determined than ever to make a difference when it came to protecting the ecosystem upon which this amazing dragon's entire species was so directly dependent.

A few days before Jake's twenty-first birthday, they felt it. A dull, low-pitched vibration resonated deep within the chests of T'Aer Bolun Dakkar and Jake. It had the insistence of a homing beacon, pulsing nonstop with an irresistible urgency that simply could not be ignored. King Tao Min Xiong was summoning them.

They left immediately, speeding toward the king's lair near the Arctic Circle. Plunging into the freezing-cold waters of the Arctic Ocean, T'Aer Bolun Dakkar quickly located the subaquatic entrance to the hidden cavern. Seconds later, they emerged inside the sacred resting place to find Tao Min Xiong there waiting for them, the glow from his scales illuminating the gold-plated walls.

Exiting the pool at the center of the expansive cavern, T'Aer Bolun Dakkar arose, standing on his hind feet and extending his wings outward to his sides as his scales began to glow. Tao Min Xiong approached, mirroring his actions as both dragons stood there, breast to breast, wing to wing, and eye to eye. This time, there was no discernable difference in their size. If anything, T'Aer Bolun Dakkar was larger. Retracting their massive wings, the two dragons partially entwined their long necks as they stood there, motionless.

After a moment, Tao Min Xiong spoke, saying, "T'Aer Bolun Dakkar, my blood is your blood. My strength is your strength. My wisdom is your wisdom. My destiny is your destiny. My kingdom is your kingdom."

Responding, T'Aer Bolun Dakkar said, "Tao Min Xiong, your blood is my blood. Your strength is my strength. Your wisdom is my wisdom. Your destiny is my destiny. Your kingdom is my kingdom."

As they parted, T'Aer Bolun Dakkar watched Tao Min Xiong turn and walk slowly toward what appeared to be a freshly excavated chamber dug deep into the wall of the cavern surrounding the tomb's watery entryway. Near the opening of the chamber, he stopped to consume half of an enormous pile of volcanic lava before backing into the narrow portal. Looking around the walls of the cavern, Jake realized there were at least a dozen such portals that had been sealed eons ago. Unlike the elevated chambers in the chimney leading up toward the surface, these portals were larger and sealed in gold from the outside.

Striking his head against the roof of his burial chamber, Tao Min Xiong caused the ceiling near the entrance to crumble, sealing the opening from the inside. Flames from within penetrated the fissures in the rubble and melted the stones until all the cracks had been sealed.

Outside the tomb, T'Aer Bolun Dakkar consumed the remaining lava. Targeting the terraces above Tao Min Xiong's chamber, he spewed superheated flames onto them, melting the thick gold plating that then flowed down the wall, covering and sealing his father's portal for eternity.

As the gold cooled, T'Aer Bolun Dakkar beckoned Jake to come nearer. Together, they pressed their right hands against the center of the portal, permanently imprinting it with their royal seals. After a short time, the pulsing sonic beacon that had so urgently summoned them began to slow, becoming fainter and fainter until it stopped. King Tao Min Xiong was dead.

After a moment of reverence before the tomb of the former king, Jake mounted T'Aer Bolun Dakkar, and the two of them departed the underwater sanctuary deep below the surface of the Arctic Ocean. Emerging from the icy black waters, T'Aer Bolun Dakkar took flight, climbing upward into the night sky. Solemnly, the two of them circled the earth at the edge of the atmosphere, in no hurry to *be* anywhere.

Looking down, Jake noticed erratic eruptions of light seeming to appear randomly across each continent as they passed over them. "What are those?" asked Jake.

"They are the glow of dragons honoring the passing of a great king," explained T'Aer Bolun Dakkar.

After crossing over each continent, subcontinent, island chain, and dragon-inhabited land mass, Jake and T'Aer Bolun Dakkar reluctantly set a course for home.

The passing of one dragon king and the ascension of another sent noticeable ripples throughout the entire community of dragons. Unlike human kingdoms, dragons did not need to defend their territory from the aggression or insurgence of other dragons. Their primary responsibility was to ensure territorial balance so as not to overpopulate any specific region, thereby placing an undue strain on territorial ecosystems.

Since dragons could survive and thrive in any climate, even under the most extreme conditions, the territorial boundaries of dragon kings had very little to do with the proximity of land masses. In fact, many dragons spent the majority of their lives underwater, surfacing only when necessary to absorb sunlight or to visit territorial breeding grounds.

Others were at home in remote regions with climatic conditions far too extreme for humans to inhabit. However, with their ability to quickly access feeding grounds located thousands of miles from their roosts, they were unaffected by local environmental conditions.

The territorial boundaries for dragons had been established eons ago by dividing the planet into four equal kingdoms: north and south of the equator and east and west of the prime meridian. While dragon kings may travel unchallenged among all four kingdoms at will, other dragons must acquire a royal seal that allowed them passage for only a limited period.

The bloodline of King Tao Min Xiong was the oldest of all dragon kings, dating back nearly one hundred million years. Because of their unique adaptability to environmental changes, they were able to survive the asteroid impact that had led to the extinction of the dinosaurs along with 90 percent of all life on Earth. With the ascension of T'Aer Bolun Dakkar and Jake, a bonded dragon and his rider now ruled the northwest dragon kingdom for the first time in over a thousand years.

Although interactions between dragons and dragon kings were extremely rare occurrences, when they were necessary, it was essential that they took place in remote, scantly populated areas. In this manner, they could avoid drawing attention that could compromise their meeting locations and lift the veil on their very existence.

For this purpose, T'Aer Bolun Dakkar and Jake selected the uninhabited Kingman Reef, a part of the Pacific Line Islands chain, south of Honolulu, as their official roost. Not surprisingly, this selection aligned perfectly with Danni's decision to complete her master of science degree in marine science at Hawaii Pacific University.

Danni's intensity in regard to her marine biology studies was surprising to all her university professors. As a young woman from Tennessee, she was surprisingly knowledgeable when it came to oceanic fish migration patterns despite the fact she'd never lived near or even visited the ocean before being accepted to the University of Miami.

Having thousands of generations of genetic memory to draw from, dragons instinctively knew where to find fish even when trawlers returned to port empty. Furthermore, they knew where *not* to fish to allow certain species the time they required to regenerate and repopulate.

T'Aer Bolun Dakkar was more than happy to share his knowledge with Danni, who was insatiable when it came to matters that could impact the delicate balance of the oceans. Through her idea exchanges with the dragon king, she had seen the accelerated decline of several species and, by dead reckoning, understood the urgent need for an immediate course change to prevent their untimely extinction.

By the time she had graduated, she was one of the world's leading authorities on oceanic fish population, migration, and reproduction, having developed a patented computer algorithm capable of accurately predicting each of those factors based on the introduction of adverse yet preventable manmade influences.

This program made it possible for researchers to determine the full impact of potential marine ventures before they were implemented and then identify specific actions that could be taken to lessen or even prevent the detrimental effects they could have on Earth's oceanic ecosystems. Her highly acclaimed patented program earned her accolades from the International Oceanic Protection Society, and her associated literary contributions earned her a nomination for the Nobel Prize for Literature.

Jake and Danni spent every possible moment together, sharing their ideas, goals, and dreams while exercising extreme care not to expose either the existence of King T'Aer Bolun Dakkar or the unseen world of dragons over which he reigned. Instead, they acted as advocates for the protection of all life on Earth by effectively applying the knowledge they had gained from him.

T'Aer Bolun Dakkar continued to enjoy the access to humans afforded him through his alter ego as Turbo and accompanied Jake everywhere he went, both in his private and official capacities.

It had been years since Svend Erickson was arrested, but in all that time, the burning curiosity he harbored toward Jake and his mysterious little Chihuahua, Turbo, never faded. After being arrested for firing an unauthorized projectile into an active flight path, the legal wrangling that had occurred resulted in a plea deal in which he and his associates received seven-year prison sentences. Since the missile had been not equipped with an explosive payload, the case for attempting to shoot down an aircraft simply couldn't be made; however, since the substance in the glass cylinder was determined to be poisonous, he and his colleagues pleaded guilty to a reduced charge of possession of a controlled substance.

The fake driver who'd held Sam, Sarah, and Madison at gunpoint before disappearing through the back door was convicted of attempted armed robbery. While Sam's interior camera system clearly showed him forcing Sam and Sarah into the dining room, both the exterior cameras covering the back and front of the house had either malfunctioned or been tampered with and hadn't captured what had actually happened outside. Nevertheless, the footage from inside the house was more than enough for a conviction.

Since the robbery had not been successful and the perpetrator hadn't fired the weapon before dropping it and attempting to flee, he received a reduced prison sentence of only ten years. Of course, he'd wasted no time when it came to providing his fellow inmates a detailed description of the event as it had actually occurred. While to most people, it may have sounded like the delirious ramblings of a psychotic lunatic, for a dragoneer, it was further proof that they were onto something and were getting close.

With their sentences now behind them, they were more convinced than ever that Turbo was indeed a dragon, and immediately after their release, the hunt was on again. What they didn't know was that Turbo was no ordinary dragon. Turbo was King T'Aer Bolun Dakkar, and they were on a collision course with the most powerful dragon to have ever roamed the earth . . . and Jake.

CHAPTER 37

DRAGONEERS WERE SINGLE-MINDEDLY focused on the pursuit of dragons. They were literally consumed by it, and nothing would ever dissuade them from their burning fanaticism. Although every dragoneer had their own motivation, Svend Erickson's was particularly polarizing.

While some dragoneers were seduced by the stories of unimaginable riches inside the lairs of dragons or the vivid tales of glory surrounding their ancestors who'd sworn an oath to rid the world of them, Svend Erickson's connection was infinitely more personal. He'd actually been a bonded rider.

Like Jake, Svend Erickson had been introduced to his dragon as a teenager. He'd been victorious in every dreamscape challenge, some of which had continued for days before finally ending in the defeat of his adversary. He'd flown to the edge of space astride the back of his dragon, Kai Bok Katari, and accompanied him to the depths of the ocean floor. He'd traveled the circumference of the earth and trained with his dragon in the fighting skills he would need to defend the kingdom to which he and Kai Bok Katari would ascend. After overcoming all obstacles during the trials of combat, he and his dragon were ready to ascend together.

Having been escorted to the final resting place for dragons in the territory of King D'Nal Rafcm, he and Kai Bok Katari were to receive the royal seal. However, while alone in the gilded cavern high atop a nameless peak in the mountains of Tibet, he failed his final test. Unable to resist the temptation of being surrounded by walls of gold and a floor plated with the glistening blood of generations of dragons, he'd taken a solid gold nugget the size of a grapefruit.

When the dragons had returned to the foyer at the entrance of the cavern, the king invited Kai Bok Katari to kneel before him and receive the royal seal. Svend Erickson, although unaware of the significance at the time, was not invited and did not receive the seal. When they left the isolated mountain peak during the whiteout conditions of a massive snowstorm, Kai Bok Katari used an undecipherable route during the return trip to the home of Svend Erickson.

That night, Svend Erickson fell into a deep dreamless sleep. When he awoke the next morning, Kai Bok Katari was gone, and while the bonding scale he'd received was still in place, the mental and emotional bond to his dragon had been completely dissolved.

The very next year, Kai Bok Katari ascended to the throne of King D'Nal Rafcm. Svend Erickson did not, and while his bond had been dissolved, his memories and heightened physical abilities had not been and served as a constant reminder of his failure. With Svend having such in-depth knowledge of the world of dragons yet no ability to access that world, his sense of loss soon became the catalyst for his outrage.

He'd spent decades searching for dragons, *any* dragons, hoping to discover the lair of a female from which he could steal an egg. Realizing there was no way he could ever reestablish the bond with now king Kai Bok Katari, his only pathway back into the world of dragons would be to bond with a newly slipped whelp. While the odds were astronomically stacked against his success, the fever ignited inside him by his craving for dragon gold was unrelenting.

During his incarceration, he used every available second to prepare for the day he'd be released. His physical workouts were insanely intense, and most other inmates avoided him completely, unsure of his intentions but well aware of his strength and agility.

His reclusive behavior didn't sit well with one of the gang leaders whom he'd openly rejected when approached for recruitment. Two days later, four of the gang members attacked him in the yard, resulting in six broken ribs, a severe concussion, two dislocated knees, and a crushed trachea, none of which belonged to Svend Erickson.

After that episode, no one dared to even speak with him during the remaining six years of his sentence. By the time he was released, only a handful of inmates had ever even heard him utter a single word, and other than the altercation in the yard, his behavior and adherence to the rules had been stellar.

It only took Svend a week to track down Jake after the steel prison gate closed behind him, and as he'd suspected, Turbo was still with him and didn't seem to have aged at all. That same night, he boarded a plane headed for Hawaii.

Realizing he'd never be able to sneak up on a dragon who'd already sensed his aura no matter how long ago it may have been, he'd lain in wait for them to leave the house under the cover of darkness. Eventually, dragons needed to feed, and he would use that opportunity to set the trap he'd been planning in his head for seven long years.

After two nights of surveilling Jake's modest beachfront home from nearly a mile away with a high-powered telescope, he spotted them as they left the house. Jake was wearing workout sweats as he and Turbo jogged down the beach to a secluded area far from the prying eyes of his closest neighbors. Moments later, he watched them take flight out over the ocean and disappear into the night sky.

They'd only been gone a few minutes before Svend broke into the house and placed two dental nitrous oxide gas canisters with remote triggers in the master bedroom upstairs, where Jake and Turbo normally slept. Afterward, he quietly crept out of the house, careful not to touch or disturb anything.

Since dental nitrous oxide gas had no detectable odor and no lasting aftereffects, he would wait until Jake was asleep before activating the remote release system. Jake would simply continue sleeping and awaken a bit later than usual, feeling only slightly groggier than he normally would.

On the other hand, the effects of nitrous oxide on a dragon were much more debilitating. T'Aer Bolun Dakkar would sleep for hours, possibly days. That would give Svend Erickson enough time to abduct and relocate him while keeping him sedated and telepathically separated from Jake.

About two hours later, Jake and T'Aer Bolun Dakkar returned, heading into the house and straight upstairs to the master bedroom, where a light came on briefly. Once the light went out, Svend waited fifteen minutes and then activated the remote release system, silently releasing the gas into the room.

Less than a minute before the gas was released into the room, Danni called. She was just leaving the baggage claim area at the airport in Nashville, having gone there to visit her parents in Tennessee.

Jake's cell phone was downstairs on the kitchen counter with his house keys. As always, whenever he heard her special ringtone, he sprinted to his phone.

Answering it, he sat on the floor in the kitchen, leaning back against the island in the center of the room, saying, "Good morning, Ms. Hawthorne."

"Good morning, Mr. Payne," she replied, smiling to herself. "Did I wake you?"

"Actually, Turbo and I just got back from our fishing trip," answered Jake, realizing Danni was well aware of what he had meant.

"I just wanted to let you know I made it," she said. "Get some sleep, sweetheart, and I'll call you later this afternoon."

"That's exactly what I'm going to do," said Jake, adding, "Tell your parents I said hello, and tell the woman in your bedroom mirror I love her and miss her already."

"Do you love her more than me?" asked Danni.

"Not a chance," said Jake. "But don't tell her I said that. I don't want her to get suspicious."

"You got it, babe. I love you too," said Danni before ending the call.

Just as Jake was about to stand up, he suddenly lost telepathic contact with T'Aer Bolun Dakkar, calling out, "Turbo, are you all right?"

There was no response.

"T'Aer Bolun Dakkar . . . Are you there?" he said aloud, sprinting up the stairs.

When he opened the door to enter the room, the gassy mist in the air briefly made his head spin. Holding his breath, he rushed into the room, opening the French doors leading out to the balcony. Turning on the ceiling fan, he was able to clear enough of the gas from the room to make the air breathable without it making him dizzy again.

Rushing over to the bed, he realized Turbo was unconscious and not responding at all to Jake's attempts to wake him. Suddenly, he heard the lock on the front door at the base of the stairs clicking open and realized what was happening. T'Aer Bolun Dakkar's identity had been discovered by someone who was now trying to abduct him.

He knew how much more effective anesthesia was on a dragon's physiology and that T'Aer Bolun Dakkar would be incapacitated for the next few hours. Stripping off his pajamas, Jake deployed his armor and placed his hand on Turbo. As he heard the intruder reach the top of the stairway outside the master bedroom, he cloaked, making himself and Turbo invisible.

Expecting both Jake and Turbo to be unconscious, Svend Erickson hadn't even bothered to wear a mask or try to conceal his identity. Jake recognized him immediately as he stood there in the doorway, looking around the room, perplexed at the absence of his targets.

Just as it had dawned on Svend that they were probably cloaked, Jake grabbed him, holding onto him tightly as he rushed toward the balcony and leapt over the railing. Both of them crashed hard onto the concrete patio below, with Svend beneath Jake, who was straddling him when they landed. Surprisingly, Svend was shaken but by no means incapacitated, having also deployed his still-functioning body armor.

Ramming his knee into Jake's ribs, Svend knocked him to the side, freeing himself. Before Jake could fully stand, Svend charged, tackling Jake into the sand on the beach behind the house. He threw several punches but was unable to connect with any of them as Jake skillfully parried every blow.

Grasping Svend's right and left arms simultaneously, Jake pulled him down while headbutting him hard, directly on the bridge of his nose, and then pushing him backward onto the sand. Before he could recover, Jake lunged, striking Svend on the point of his chin with his right knee.

Svend landed facedown in the sand and tried to push himself up. Jake reacted quickly, leaping onto the center of Svend's back, driving both knees hard into his spine and flattening him into the sand again. Grabbing both of Svend's arms and pulling them back, Jake flipped onto his back, taking Svend with him. Locking his legs into the crooks of Svend's elbows, Jake wrapped his left arm around Svend's neck and the right arm over the top of his head in a classic sleeper hold.

No matter how hard Svend struggled, he was unable to free himself as Jake's iron grip remained tightly locked across his neck, cutting off the blood flow to Svend's oxygen-starved brain. Svend continued to flail about; however, the battle had already been lost. Even with his body armor deployed, he was hopelessly outmatched.

Jake was unbelievably strong, applying enough pressure to overpower Svend's body armor, armor capable of withstanding the oceanic pressures of the Mariana Trench. After Svend struggled for several minutes, his resistance slowly waned under Jake's uncompromising grip.

Jake maintained that grip for a while, even after Svend's resistance had ended, realizing how the armor itself could store enough oxygen to revive him even after having his airways cut off for an extended period. When Jake finally released his iron grip, kicking Svend's unresponsive body over to the side, he knelt beside the oblivious dragoneer, confirming he still had a pulse before walking down to the water's edge.

From the moonlit beach, Jake summoned King Kai Bok Katari, who arrived in fewer than twenty minutes. As the visiting dragon king landed on the beach near Jake, there were no words exchanged between the two of them. Grasping the situation immediately, the visiting king collected the unconscious body of his former bonded rider and disappeared with him into the dark night sky. Kai Bok Katari would be the dragon king who would ultimately decide the fate of his former bonded rider; however, it was certain he would never be allowed to pursue dragons in *any* dragon kingdom ever again.

Rushing back into the house, Jake discovered and removed the empty nitrous oxide canisters from beneath the head of his bed. Turbo was still sleeping soundly as Jake crawled back into bed beside him. He would inform King T'Aer Bolun Dakkar of what had transpired once his bonded dragon had fully regained his intellectual faculties. As the sun began peeking over the horizon to the east, Jake was finally able to sense T'Aer Bolun Dakkar's telepathic connection again, and after only a few minutes, he was also sound asleep.

Turbo awakened late in the afternoon and made his way downstairs on wobbly legs. Jake was outside on the patio, using his laptop to work with Danni on a presentation for the World Health Organization, when Turbo joined him.

"Good afternoon," said Jake, smiling. "I'm glad you've decided to join us."

"Good afternoon, Turbo," said Danni, waving from the video conference window on Jake's laptop screen.

"Good afternoon, Danni. Good afternoon, Jake," replied T'Aer Bolun Dakkar, still visibly groggy and unaware of what had transpired. "I feel as if I could have slept for days."

"Actually, you slept for three," replied Jake.

To T'Aer Bolun Dakkar's complete and utter astonishment, Jake recounted the details missing from the dragon king's memory.

After his initial shock had dissipated, T'Aer Bolun Dakkar realized the full extent of Jake's courage and abilities, saying, "I'm proud of you, Jake. King Tao Min Xiong showed great wisdom in selecting you as my bond."

That night, the four dragon kings convened at T'Aer Bolun Dakkar's roost in the Line Islands to discuss the fate of the disgraced Svend Erickson. Dragons did not kill humans or other dragons, and only the king of a former bonded rider may decide that rider's ultimate fate. In light of his obsession for dragon gold, the four kings reached a consensus to grant Svend Erickson's incessant wish.

At the conclusion of their brief meeting, Jake and T'Aer Bolun Dakkar took custody of a bound Svend Erickson, allowing him to once again experience the rush of flight with a dragon. They flew without urgency, allowing Svend to absorb the beauty of the world from a dragon's perspective at the edge of the atmosphere.

After crossing over the North Pole, they descended into the icy waters of the Arctic Ocean, diving deep into its chilling black depths. They swam slowly, allowing Svend Erickson the opportunity to see exactly where he was being taken. It also gave him the opportunity to assess the sheer impossibility of him ever negotiating this route without the escort of King T'Aer Bolun Dakkar.

Entering the opening near the ocean floor, they ascended slowly for a dragon—but impossibly fast for even the most capable human being—into the gilded burial grounds of the ancestors of T'Aer Bolun Dakkar. As they emerged from the lagoon inside the secluded cavern, T'Aer Bolun Dakkar's scales lit up, illuminating the gold-encrusted walls and floor and revealing that which had driven Svend Erickson over the brink of insanity.

Removing two oversized waterproof duffel bags from T'Aer Bolun Dakkar's back, Jake placed them on the elevated floor in the center of the cavern. Inside them were enough supplies to comfortably sustain the rider-turned-dragoneer for several weeks. After releasing him from his constraints, Jake left him there near the supplies and turned to walk back toward T'Aer Bolun Dakkar.

As Svend finally realized the nightmare ahead of him, the gravity of his punishment sank in. This would be his prison for the remainder of his life, surrounded by the gold he so desperately craved yet unable to remove even a single ounce of it or leave the dragon graveyard that would eventually be his own.

In an act of final desperation, he charged toward Jake. Sensing the attack, Jake turned, quickly gripping Svend Erickson by the neck with his right hand and lifting him into the air before tossing him back onto the elevated ground near the supplies.

"We will return periodically with fresh supplies for you, but you will never leave this place to hunt dragons or their bonded riders ever again," stated Jake, mounting the back of T'Aer Bolun Dakkar. "There are LED lanterns packed at the very top of each duffel bag. Twisting the crank on the side recharges them, and they'll provide sufficient light for several hours. There are no batteries and nothing flammable inside the bags but pretty much everything else you'll need to survive comfortably until we return."

Jake and T'Aer Bolun Dakkar dove back into the watery portal, leaving Svend Erickson alone in the solitary confinement of the dragon graveyard.

CHAPTER 38

THE TRAJECTORY OF life is often unpredictable. For Big Sam, it was especially so. Having accepted an offer from Madison McClure to serve as the regional foreman, he was now in charge of MTAC's statewide operations. After putting farmers back in charge of their own agricultural destinies, MTAC had morphed into a very effective farming co-op.

Working with farmers across the state, they were able to increase their total yield by promoting effective crop rotation among participating farms. By offering a selection of crops farmers could choose from and guaranteeing top market prices for their produce, MTAC helped farmers maximize their production volume while minimizing soil depletion. As a result, they were consistently able to bring an abundance of high-quality produce to the market and ensure the farmers received top dollar for the fruits of their labors.

MTAC also provided education, training, and man power assistance for farmers who might be planting crops with which they weren't as familiar, thus eliminating their apprehensions regarding crop rotation. Working hand in hand with those farmers, they were also able to match labor personnel to crops with which they were experienced in harvesting while providing fair and uniform compensation for them.

Needless to say, under Big Sam's management, MTAC was turning huge profits without taking unfair advantage of the farmers working with them. Within seven years, his business model was being used by farmers and agricultural corporations across the country.

After only a brief conversation with T'Aer Bolun Dakkar, Danni Hawthorne's passion for the preservation of the planet's oceanic ecosystems had been awakened. Her dedication to this cause had literally altered the way scientists viewed and responded to the changes in the earth's oceanic biosphere.

For many people, the search for their purpose, their calling, and their destiny could take a lifetime of consideration and soul searching. It involved years of starting, failing, and starting all over again without losing that sense of passion that inspired them to do great things.

However, when a great need arose, a champion would appear. While some were moved by unexpected success or unanticipated disaster, for others, it only took a second glance at something small yet extraordinary that had been there all along.

For Jake . . . it took a dragon.

The End

CPSIA information can be obtained
at www.ICGtesting.com
Printed in the USA
FFHW021805260919
55235613-60966FF